DUE PROCESS

DUE PROCESS

By

SCOTT PRATT

ISBN: 1944083022
ISBN 13: 9781944083021

ACKNOWLEDGEMENTS

Thank you to Don Spurrell and Jim Bowman, both great friends and excellent lawyers. They're my go-to guys when I have a question about law. And thank you to Dr. Kenneth Ferslew for helping me understand the effects of GHB and the procedures involved in its detection.

This book, along with every book I've written and every book I'll write, is dedicated to my darling Kristy, to her unconquerable spirit and to her inspirational courage. I loved her before I was born and I'll love her after I'm long gone.

PART ONE

FRIDAY, AUGUST 23

My name is Joe Dillard, and it was hot and muggy outside as I drove my wife's car northeast through Knoxville on our way back home from Nashville. My wife, Caroline, was in the passenger seat, sleeping. I was listening to a podcast called "S-Town" about a bi-polar, suicidal genius in Alabama who probably suffered from mercury poisoning and may or may not have hid-den a bunch of gold on his property.

I was listening to the podcast primarily to keep my mind off of what was going on with Caroline. The drugs that had been controlling her metastatic breast cancer had once again stopped working – the cancer was advancing in her liver – and she'd been placed in a clinical trial at Vanderbilt University in Nashville. The trial was studying the effectiveness of an immunother-apy drug that had not yet been approved by the Food and Drug Administration. She'd been on the drug for almost two months and had tolerated it fairly well. It had also shrunk the tumors in her liver, but other drugs had done the same thing, and, like lethal soldiers, the cancer eventually found a way to improvise, adapt and overcome.

She'd also recently had to have radiation on her left knee because a cancerous tumor had wrapped itself around the joint and the doctors said they were afraid the knee would snap. I wouldn't wish radiation on my worst enemy after seeing its effects on Caroline in the past. She'd had her breast radiated initially, and that put her down for several months. Later, after the metastasis, she'd had her entire spine radiated, which nearly killed her. After that, they'd radiated her brain to keep the cancer cells from getting in there. The brain radiation had left her unable to function for months.

And now they'd told us that an MRI of Caroline's brain showed the beginnings of cancer in her cerebellum, which is the part of the brain that controls balance and movement. I found that ironic and tragic, because she had been a dancer and dance teacher all of her life. The neurologist had assured us that it could be handled with radiosurgery (precisely-targeted radiation) and that there would be no side effects, but I hated the thought of Caroline going through more radiation. I hated that the disease had emaciated her, that it had taken her beautiful hair, that it had caused her so much pain and worry and heartache. I hated that she had to rely on so many drugs to survive. I hated the relentlessness of it all. I'd come to hate cancer with a passion I could not begin to adequately describe.

The worst part of the clinical trial was that we had to drive to Nashville two out of every three weeks, and Nashville was a five-hundred-and-fifty-mile round trip from our home in Johnson City. We also had to spend the night in a hotel each time, so it was expensive. Caroline told me we were spending a little over a thousand dollars a month for hotels, gas and meals, but I wasn't really concerned about the expense. We were in good shape financially, and even if we weren't, I would have spent my last dime if it helped make her feel better and prolonged her life.

She woke up as we entered Knoxville, just like she always did. The nurses at Vanderbilt gave her Benadryl during her immune-drug infusion, and it always put her to sleep. She slept through the infusion, woke up long enough to get to the car, and then slept another two-and-a-half hours until we got to Knoxville.

I looked over at her when she said, "What are you listening to?"

"It's called 'Shit Town,'" I said.

"Classy title."

"It actually fits. You'd have to listen to it to understand. You want me to turn it off and put on some music?"

"Please. I don't think I can handle Shit Town right now."

"Country?"

"Is there anything else?"

Caroline had become a huge fan of modern country music. It had come out of the blue a few years earlier. She'd spent her entire life listening to pop – the same music the majority of her dance students listened to – but one day she heard a cross-over country song that she loved, and she'd been listening to country ever since. Her favorite artist was Carrie Underwood, who Caroline said had perfected her own genre called "vigilante country." I'd listened to some of Ms. Underwood's music and had to agree with Caroline's classification of the genre. Carrie Underwood had probably killed off more men in her songs than any other artist I'd ever heard. I wondered why Caroline loved the lyrics so much, though. I'd asked her whether I should start watching my back.

As we approached one of the exits not far from the University of Tennessee, Caroline said, "You know what? I could use a beer."

Caroline rarely drank, so the statement was a surprise.

"Are you asking me to stop and get you a beer?"

"No. I'm asking you to stop and get me a six-pack. Get those little ones. What are they, seven ounces?"

"Yeah, seven ounces. What brought on this sudden thirst for beer?"

"I don't know. Maybe it's the trial drug. But I want to drink a few beers."

"Do you think it'll be good for you?" I said.

"C'mon, Joe. I have cancer in my bones, my liver and my brain. I've had it for years. I've taken every drug known to man. Do you seriously think a couple of beers is going to matter?"

I couldn't argue with that, so I pulled off I-40, went into a convenience store, and bought a six-pack of seven-ounce Bud Light bottles. I opened one, handed it to her, and headed back onto the interstate. She was digging in the bag for a second beer by the time I merged onto the highway.

"Are we breaking the law?" she said.

"Do you mean are *you* breaking the law? I'm not drinking in the car."

"Well, am I?"

"Would it make you feel good if you were?"

"It'd make me feel naughty. I don't get a chance to be naughty much these days."

"Sorry to disappoint you," I said, "but a passenger can drink a beer in the great state of Tennessee."

"I'm disappointed."

"You can pretend you're naughty. Use your imagination."

The second bottle went down almost as quickly as the first.

"You're slamming that stuff," I said. "You looking to get drunk?"

She took OxyContin for pain every day, she'd taken the Benadryl earlier, and she was already reaching for her third beer.

"I need to talk to you," she said.

"And you can't do it sober?"

"I'd rather not."

"Okay… talk."

"You've been dreaming about me dying, Joe. You're having nightmares about it."

What she was saying was true. She'd awakened me several times over the past month, but I had no idea she knew the specifics of the dreams I'd been having.

"I'm sorry," I said. "I'm talking in my sleep?"

"You've always talked when you have nightmares, and you sweat so much the sheets get soaked. You've been having nightmares about Sarah, too, about when she was raped when you were children."

"What do you want me to say, Caroline? I don't have them intentionally."

"Do you think I'm going to die?"

"No."

"Do you want me to die? Are you tired of all this? Because I'd understand if you are. I read about this syndrome last week. It's called compassion fatigue. I think you have it."

"Did you just ask me if I want you to die? I'm not even going to answer the question. I'll just chalk it up to the drugs and the beer. And I've never heard of compassion fatigue."

"I'm not drunk and I've taken so many drugs they don't even affect me. Look up compassion fatigue when we get home. It happens to a lot of different groups of people, like nurses and doctors and police officers, but one of the other groups is caregivers within families who have to deal with the long-term illness of a relative or a spouse. You're definitely in that category."

"So? Are you saying I don't care anymore?"

"I'm saying you're tired of all this and it's stressing you out to the point that you're having nightmares."

"I think you're wrong."

"I'm not wrong. You're losing compassion. You're becoming numb. You're doing it to protect yourself because you're afraid I'm going to die."

"Fine," I said. I was starting to get angry but trying very hard to control the emotion. "But this isn't fair. Seriously, how dare you suggest that I want you to die? So you have cancer. That doesn't mean you can do or say whatever you want. Sometimes you think there are no longer any consequences to your behavior because you can always play the cancer card."

"See?" she said, her voice rising. "That's exactly what I'm talking about. You're mean to me. You were never mean to me before."

As much as I hated it, this kind of spat was becoming more frequent between us. There always seemed to be tension hanging over us. I knew it was the constant pressure and frustration from the disease, but that didn't make it any less real. And as much as I didn't want to admit it, there was probably at least a grain of truth to what she was saying. I thought she was wrong about any lack of compassion, but the more time that passed and the more the disease progressed, the more stress I felt. I found myself wondering what I would do without her, and I didn't have any answers. But I couldn't say that out loud, I couldn't talk to her about it, because I knew if I started talking about what I'd do without her, I'd start tearing up and might even cry, and that would just upset her more. As far as the nightmares went, she was probably right. The long-term stress of dealing with the disease was a contributing factor, but my confusion about and fear of having to go on living without the woman I'd loved since I was a teenager was also undoubtedly in the mix.

"Can we please not argue?" I said. "I love you. I've always loved you and I will continue to love you. I'm sorry about the nightmares, I really am. I'll sleep on the couch so I won't wake you."

"I don't want you to sleep on the couch. I want you to sleep in our bed like you always have."

"Then I'll sleep in our bed like I always have."

She took another pull off a beer and turned toward me.

"Why are you suddenly being so agreeable?"

"Look," I said. "This has been a long, hard road for both of us. For all of us. Especially for you. And now that Lilly and Randy and Joseph are gone, it's been even harder. We don't have as much help, and I've seen an emptiness in you that breaks my heart. You and Lilly were always so close, and we both had so much fun with Joseph. When they left, it was like part of your heart was torn out of your chest. Mine, too, but it's been worse for you."

My son-in-law, Randy Lowe, had graduated from medical school and was now in an oncology residency program at the Dana-Farber Cancer Institute in Boston. Caroline and I loved Randy deeply and were both extremely proud of him, but at the same time, we resented him for taking our beloved daughter and grandson to Boston. Caroline looked at me and tears filled her eyes.

"But you're still here," she said, "and I have Jack and Charlie. I just hate the thought that I'm causing you to have nightmares. And I thought the thing with Sarah was put to rest a long time ago."

"I guess it'll never be put to rest," I said. "I don't know why I'm dreaming about it, but let's just do what we've always done. Let's just hang in there and keep loving each other."

She leaned across the seat and kissed me on the cheek.

"I love you," she said.

"I love you, too," I said. "Hand me one of those beers. We'll be naughty together."

SUNDAY, AUGUST 25

"**I** was raped," the girl said in a voice that could barely be heard. The Johnson City Police Officer, Tonya James, looked into her rearview mirror.

"What did you say?"

Officer James had put her passenger, a redhead who gave the name of Sheila Self and said she was twenty-four years old but didn't have any identification, into the back seat of her cruiser five minutes earlier at a convenience store on Walnut Street not far from East Tennessee State University. It was 1:30 a.m. on a Sunday morning. The passenger wore a tight, short, red spandex dress, spiked heels, heavy make-up, and looked like a hooker. Ms. Self was under the influence of some substance or was, perhaps, mentally ill. She initially made absolutely no sense at all when Officer James showed up after responding to a 911 call that reported Ms. Self was wandering around inside the convenience store muttering to herself and had refused to leave. After speaking to Ms. Self for several minutes and consulting her supervisor, Officer James determined that an involuntary mental health commitment may be in order, and she was transporting Ms. Self to Woodlawn Mental Health Facility for an evaluation.

"Do you know where I'm taking you?" Officer James asked.

"Woodlawn, but I'm not cra… crazy. I was drugged and raped."

"Raped? When?"

"Not really sure. Hour ago, maybe? Longer?"

The woman's speech was slurred and she smelled of alcohol, but this was the first time she'd mentioned drugs or being raped. Officer James needed to pay attention in case it was true.

"Do you know who raped you?"

"Some guys, maybe three. They puh…pulled me into a bathroom."

"Where did this happen?"

"Party. Tree Streets."

Officer James pulled into a church parking lot, turned toward the back seat, and gave her passenger her full attention.

"Tell me what happened."

"I went there to dance. I work for AAA Escort. Sometimes I do exotic dancing. They set it up."

"What time were you supposed to be there?"

"Midnight."

"And you got there at midnight?"

"I think I took a cab. It's still fuzzy, but some of it's starting to come back to me."

"Do you know the names of any of the people who raped you?"

"No."

"Can you describe them?"

"Not really. Not right now. It was dark."

"Were they white or black or Hispanic or Indian or Asian? Can you tell me their race?"

"At least one of them was black. They were football players."

"Football players? How do you know that?"

"Football player party. The escort service told me. The guy that paid me said he was a captain."

Officer James found it interesting that the young woman was suddenly recalling some details, but nothing that could really help the police find who committed the rape, if a rape had really been committed.

"Who paid you?"

"Some big guy."

"Was he one of the men that raped you?"

"I'm not sure."

"How did he pay you?"

"Cash money."

"Do you have the money?"

"Did you go through my purse?"

"Yes."

"Was it in there?"

"No."

"Then I don't know what happened to it. One of them probably stole it. Maybe I lost it."

"How many people were at this party?"

"I don't know. A bunch, I think."

"How much did you get paid?"

"Three hundred. I split with the escort service, which means I would've made a hundred and fifty. I usually get tips, but not tonight. And the escort service is going to be pissed when I go in there empty handed."

She's thinking clearly enough to do the math on her money, Officer James thought. *And now she's worrying about consequences from the escort service.*

"So you got there at midnight?"

"Yeah, I think so."

"Did you dance?"

"I started, but it went wrong somehow. Next thing I know I was in that bathroom and they were raping me."

"Did they beat you? Did they have weapons?"

"They just trained me."

"Trained you?"

"Just one after another. I didn't fight. I was scared. It's like a dream."

"Do you have any serious injuries?" Officer James asked.

"I don't think so. I'm sore down there, but they didn't hurt me bad."

"How did you get out of the house?"

"I think I walked."

"So they just let you go?"

"When they were done."

Officer James didn't quite know what to think. She took out a note pad and jotted several things down while they were fresh in her memory.

"I'm going to have to take you to the hospital, Ms. Self. You're going to need to do a rape kit, talk to the nurse and the doctor, and I'm going to get in touch with a detective and he'll be there to talk to you, too."

"He? Don't you have a woman who can talk to me?"

"Not right now. We had a woman on the detective squad, but she got married and moved away a couple of months ago. Right now, all we have are men. We're not a very big department."

"Don't take me to Woodlawn. I'm not crazy. And I have babies at home."

"Babies? How old are your babies?"

"Two and three. My cousin is keeping them tonight."

"So they'll be all right? Do you want to call your cousin?"

"They're asleep. I'll see her in the morning."

"Have you ever been through a rape examination before, Ms. Self?"

"Yes."

"You have? When?"

"My stepfather raped me when I was young. Then my foster father and brother both raped me. I've been through it twice."

Officer James shook her head, not knowing whether what she was hearing was the truth. If it was, then the person she was carrying in her back seat had to have some serious psychological baggage.

"I'm sorry to hear that," Officer James said. "At least you know what you're about to go through. You know it isn't going to be fun. But it's extremely important. So just be brave and do what the medical people tell you to do, okay?"

"I can handle it."

Officer James turned her blue lights on and did a U-turn in the parking lot. Twenty minutes ago, this woman could barely talk, or at least that's the way she was acting. Now, she seemed far more lucid and was telling a tale, albeit an unusual one, of being gang-raped.

James called her supervisor.

"She claims she was raped," James said. "The plan has changed. I'm going to take her to the medical center."

SUNDAY, AUGUST 25

Investigator Bo Riddle was dreaming of putting the noose around the neck of a black man named Howard Felts when his cell phone began to buzz on the bedside table. Riddle had been instrumental in convicting Felts of murder a week earlier, and the jury had later come back with a death penalty sentence. A thirty-year-old patrol officer with a wife and two young daughters had responded to a domestic disturbance at Felts' apartment eighteen months earlier, and as soon as the patrolman walked through the door, Felts ambushed him and shot him in the face. Felts had never shown a bit of remorse and had been a terrible disciplinary problem at the jail and in the courtroom for the past year-and-a-half. As soon as the verdict was announced, he'd been shipped off to Death Row at Riverbend in Nashville, which, Riddle believed, was exactly where he belonged. The only problem was that he'd be on Death Row for fifteen years. Riddle believed death penalty sentences should be carried out on a flatbed truck in front of the courthouse in the county where the crime was committed. And forget the appeals process. The man was tried and convicted by a jury and that same jury sentenced him to death. End of story.

It was 6:30 a.m. on Sunday morning, and Riddle would have rolled out of bed in fifteen minutes, so the hour didn't annoy him. But the interruption of the dream did. It was one of the better dreams Riddle had experienced in a while.

He picked up the phone and growled, "What?"

The voice on the other end of the phone was Tonya James, a five-year patrol veteran of the JCPD.

"There's a woman who claims she was gang-raped by at least three ETSU football players at a party last night," James said.

"And?"

"The watch commander wants you to take the interview and get a statement. I took her to the hospital and they did a rape kit. They're just finishing up, but she's a little strange. There were some problems with her story."

"What kind of problems?"

"Details. Important things. Like what time she arrived at the party, what time she was raped, how long she was raped, what time she left, exactly how many attackers there were. She can't describe them. Then there's the fact that she'd been hired to strip at the party."

"Sounds to me like you don't believe her," Riddle said.

"She didn't mention being raped until she figured out I was taking her to Woodlawn for a mental evaluation. I ran her name through a couple of databases and talked to a guy at the Carter County Sheriff's Department because she lives over there. She's had some problems in the past. The guy I talked to in Carter County thinks she's got a screw loose."

"So she has mental issues? Has she been committed?"

"A couple of times, both involuntary and short term. I don't have official confirmation of that, no records. Just going by what my guy in Carter County told me."

"And who is your guy?"

"I talked to the Chief Deputy of the Sheriff's Department. Name's Clinton Drake. Known him a long time. Good guy."

"Yeah, I know Drake," Riddle said. "Does this woman have a criminal record?"

"Minor stuff. Drug and alcohol related. She's on probation for a possession charge right now, plus she has one D.U.I. and two public intoxication charges. Drake said she came up really rough. Sexual abuse by her father. Mother wouldn't intervene. She was removed from her home when she was fourteen and the father went to prison, but then she was raped by a foster father and a foster brother. The foster father went to prison. The brother went to juvy."

"Good God," Riddle said. "She must be the personification of jail bait."

"She's good looking. I spent a couple of hours talking to her. She's been a stripper since she was eighteen and has done some hooking through the escort service. She has two young kids but no man. What's weird is that she managed to earn an associate's degree from a junior college and is enrolled at ETSU part-time."

"What is she majoring in?" Riddle said.

"Psychology. I guess she's trying to figure some things out."

"Who's doing the rape kit?" Riddle asked.

"A nurse named Franklin and a doctor named Bosco. Don't know either one of them, and they don't seem too friendly. So how about getting here as soon as possible and helping me out? I don't want this woman to get away. She might be nuts, but she might have been raped. If she was, I want whoever raped her held accountable."

"I'll call Judge Murphy and go by his house. We need an order for a blood draw that we can send to an independent lab for Drug Facilitated Sexual Assault analysis," Riddle said. "The TBI isn't set up for that kind of test. I'm sure they've done a tox screen, but from what you've told me, that might not be enough. We're going to need to know exactly what was in her system and how much."

"I already did that," James said. "I did it as soon as I brought her in and they started the exam. I didn't go to Murphy, though. I woke up Judge Tinker. He'll sign anything and he's friendlier than Murphy. I figured we'd need the blood before so much time passed they couldn't get a reliable result from the test. They drew the blood about 2:30 a.m., two-and-a-half hours after this alleged party."

"Well, aren't you just an up and comer?" Riddle said. "Nice work. I can be there in about thirty minutes, but don't get too close to me because I'm not gonna take a shower."

Riddle arrived at the emergency room exactly thirty minutes after he hung up the phone.

"Morning," Tonya James said. She introduced Riddle to Sheila Self, who was sitting in a chair wearing a paper gown covered by blankets. Riddle was immediately struck by how pretty she was, although it was a rough kind of pretty. He guessed she was quite a bit younger than she looked. Still, she had long, striking red hair and clear, blue eyes, cream-colored skin and full, sensuous lips.

"I'm going to talk to Officer James out in the hall for a minute, Miss Self," Riddle said. "I'll be right back. Just sit tight."

"What do the nurse and doc say?" Riddle said when he and James were outside.

"The nurse told me the vic had definitely been involved in sexual activity. There was some swelling of the vagina and a couple of bruises, but the bruises were minor. No cuts, no tearing of the vagina or anus. She obviously didn't fight them, or at least she didn't fight them hard, and they didn't beat her. The rape examiners got a bunch of hairs and fibers and she had sperm in her, so there will be DNA."

"What did the nurse say about rape?"

"She said it was possible."

"Possible? Is that a strong possible? A probable? Or anything is possible?"

James shook her head. "I pressed her, but that's as far as she'd go."

"What about the doctor?"

"He left at six. The nurse said he'd tell me the same thing, though. Based on their observations, the swelling, the sperm, the bruising, and the victim's account, it's possible that a rape occurred."

"Talk to the vic any more about descriptions, who the perps might have been?"

"She said somebody gave her a drink when she got there and it must have had something in it. She said she doesn't remember much after the drink. I asked her to sign a consent form so we could get a copy of her tox screen and see what kind of drugs or how much alcohol she had in her when I brought her in, but she wouldn't sign it."

"Doesn't really matter if we got blood for the DFSA," Riddle said, "but I think I can get a look at it anyway."

"How's that?"

"I've been at this a long time, James. I have friends in low places."

James shrugged.

"She's not a suspect in a crime unless maybe it's for filing a false report, so I guess there's no harm in you going around the rules. It isn't like we're going to use the results against her in court."

"Right," Riddle said. "You can take off now. I'll handle it from here."

Riddle walked back into the room where Sheila Self was sitting. She hadn't moved.

"Can I get you anything?" Riddle said.

"A different life," Sheila said.

"I think we all wish for that once in a while," Riddle said. "Yours truly included. But sometimes we're stuck with what we have. We make the best of it, right?"

"I wish I could talk to a woman detective."

"Sorry, we're fresh out. Looks like you'll have to deal with me, but I'm not such a bad guy once you get to know me. I'm sure this has to be difficult, but I need to hear everything you can remember about last night.

What you've described to Officer James is aggravated kidnapping and aggravated rape. Those are extremely serious charges. If we can identify the men who did it and they're tried and convicted, they'll go to prison for a long time."

"They should go to prison," Sheila said quietly. "They deserve to go to prison."

"When did you first find out about the party?" Riddle said.

"My escort service called me Friday afternoon around five. Asked if I could dance at this party last night on Elm Street. I said I'd do it and I called my cousin to see if she'd keep my kids. I told her I had a date. She said yes, so I was good to go. She picked my kids up about six."

"She picked your kids up from where?"

"My apartment."

"A man live with you?"

"No. Just the kids. We live in Section 8 housing over by the Tweetsie Trail. I get food stamps, Aid for Dependent Children, all that. I go to school part time and I dance and work for the escort service on the side. It's decent money sometimes."

"But you don't declare any of it, right? Are you a prostitute as well?"

"No. I'm a dancer and an escort. Whose side are you on here?"

"Just doing my job. No offense. And you got to the party when?"

"Around midnight."

"How'd you get there?"

"I already told the other officer. I took a cab from my apartment."

"What did you do between six and midnight?"

"My boyfriend came over and we partied a little."

"What's your boyfriend's name?"

"I'd rather not say."

"I need to know his name."

"Bobby Vines."

"Did you have sex?"

"That's none of your business."

"You're a real peach," Riddle said. "I'm trying to help you and you're jerking me around. The nurse told the officer who brought you in here they found sperm in you. It'd be good to know if this sperm came from your boyfriend."

"It might have."

"Fine. Okay. Did your boyfriend know you were going to strip at a party at midnight, and if so, what did he think about it?"

"He doesn't care. He knows I have to make money to take care of my kids and pay my rent. He doesn't give me money."

"Is he the father of your children?"

"No."

"Who is?"

"I'm not sure."

That's great. That's just grand, Riddle thought to himself. *This is getting better by the second. She'll be such a sympathetic victim in front of a jury.*

"I understand you're on probation for a drug possession charge. What was the drug?"

"What difference does it make?"

"You're really starting to piss me off, you know that? I can find out, but that's extra work and you making me do extra work would make me feel not so sympathetic toward you. You want to do it that way?"

"It was heroin."

"So you did some heroin last night before you went to dance?"

"No, no heroin. I did some ecstasy and I drank two beers and did a shot of tequila. After I got to the party, somebody handed me a drink, though, and I think there might have been something in it. I lost it after that. Just really lost it, you know? All I have are flashes of memory. I can see hands on my arm pulling me into the bathroom. I can hear the music playing and people hollering."

"This hand on your arm, was it white or black?"

"It was black."

"So you remember that? Are you sure?"

"Pretty sure."

"On a scale of one to ten, how sure?"

"Seven or eight."

"Was there a light on in the bathroom?"

"I don't think so. Maybe some light filtering through the window from outside, but I can't say for sure."

"Did these guys talk to you? Did they talk at all? Did you hear any names?"

"I think they were talking a little, calling me bitch and slut. Talking dirty."

"Did you see a weapon of any kind?"

"I think I remember one of them had a broom and said he was going to stick the handle in me."

"Did he?"

"I don't know. Maybe."

"Were you in a lot of pain?"

"I don't know. Whatever was in the drink, the molly, the alcohol, all of it combined ... I was pretty messed up."

"Are you in a lot of pain now?"

"Not really."

"So you don't know if you cried out for help?"

"I don't know."

"Did anyone try to help you?"

"I don't think so."

"How long were you in the bathroom?"

"Long enough for the three of them to do what they wanted to do, I guess."

"So when the lab analyzes this rape kit, besides your boyfriend, they're going to find sperm or pubic hairs or something else containing DNA from three different males in you or on you, and those males will more than likely be ETSU football players?"

"I guess."

"You guess? That's not very encouraging, Miss Self. And when it was over, what happened?"

"I don't remember. I started coming to after that officer arrested me and put me in the back seat of her car. I think I was at a convenience store, but I don't really know how I got there or what I was doing there."

"Did you ever actually dance?"

"I think I started, but it didn't last long. There might have been some kind of argument. They maybe wanted me to use toys or whatever, but I didn't have anything like that. They started hollering and calling me names and I think I just told them to go screw themselves, I was leaving. That's when I got grabbed up and pulled into the bathroom."

"So you remember that? You remember starting the dance, them calling you names, and you telling them to screw themselves? And then you remember being pulled into the bathroom?"

"I think so. Vaguely."

"And again, you think it was a black hand that pulled your arm?"

Sheila nodded.

"Anything else you can remember about the guy that pulled you in? Long hair or short hair? Anything about his face? How big was he?"

She shook her head. "I'm sorry. Maybe it will come back to me later."

"The others?"

"Not really."

"When did you realize you'd been raped?"

"In the back of the police car, I think."

"So that's why you didn't report it, correct?"

"I was drugged. Somebody had to drug me."

"Ms. Self, it would help me a lot if I could get your consent to look at the toxicology screen." He decided not to tell her that some of the blood they'd drawn from her was already headed for a lab.

She shook her head vigorously.

"You can't. I'm on probation."

"But if you took the drugs involuntarily, your probation—"

"I didn't take the ecstasy involuntarily."

"Your probation officer doesn't know that, and I won't tell him."

"Her."

"Okay. I won't tell her. You can say the ecstasy was in the same drink as the other drug, whatever it turns out to be. Will any heroin show up on the tox screen?"

"No, I've been clean."

"Okay, there you go. I'll back you up on your claim that it's probable that the ecstasy and whatever else they found were mixed in the same drink. No probation violation. You give me consent to look at your tox screen and it ups your credibility as a witness a ton. What do you think?"

Sheila looked at the ground, then up at Riddle. Riddle was again taken aback by her sexuality. To him, she had a strange kind of vibe going, very sexy. The kind of woman you wanted to protect and ravage at the same time. She reminded him of a teenage girl he knew, a close friend of his daughter's. He'd been divorced from his first wife for ten years and didn't see that much of his daughter, but sometimes, when she came over on a weekend, she brought this friend named Lisa with her. Lisa was a sixteen-year-old version of Sheila, although she came from a wealthy family and would be going to college instead of a foster home. But Riddle always found himself wanting to protect Lisa as much as he wanted to protect his own daughter. He'd also fantasized about Lisa, sexual fantasies that had awakened him at night. He knew he shouldn't be fantasizing about this teenaged girl, but Riddle didn't feel guilty. It was what it was. He was old and horny, she was young and sexy, and his daughter kept bringing her around. It wasn't his fault.

Finally, Sheila nodded her head.

"I guess I don't have any choice," she said. "Once this gets out, and I'm sure it'll get out, I guess my probation officer will get the records anyway."

"Don't worry about it," Riddle said. "Investigator Riddle will take care of you."

"Just promise me you'll get the people who raped me," Sheila said.

"I'll do my best, ma'am," Riddle said. "I give you my word. But you need to come to the station and give me a written statement. Can you come after you get out of here?"

"I need to deal with my kids."

"Okay. After lunch, then. Let's exchange numbers, and I'll see you this afternoon."

SUNDAY, AUGUST 25

"**C**offee?"

Johnson City Police Chief Gene Starring looked up at Investigator Riddle from his kitchen table. It was Sunday morning, 9:00 a.m. Riddle had called and said he needed to talk to him right away, face-to-face. Starring was a twenty-five-year veteran of the police force and had been chief for nine years. He was lean and handsome, salt-and-pepper hair, well known for his self-discipline. Riddle knew the chief ate two thousand calories a day, got up at four every morning, ran five miles, spent another hour in the gym, and abstained from alcohol, tobacco, and anything else that Riddle might consider fun. Starring was fifty, but he looked like he was in his late thirties. He had an impeccable reputation for integrity, and was respected by the employees who served with him. Even Riddle respected him, albeit grudgingly.

"Thanks," Riddle said. "I could use a little shot in the arm."

Starring got up, poured a cup, and handed it to Riddle.

"My only vice," Starring said.

"What, coffee?"

"Caffeine. But I only drink one cup a day, at nine o'clock in the morning."

"Some people would say that's weird," Riddle said.

"It *is* weird," Starring said. "I'm weird, but it doesn't make me a bad person, does it?"

"Guess not."

"So, what's up?" the chief said. "You sounded a little rattled over the phone."

"The watch commander had me go to the hospital to interview an alleged rape victim this morning," Riddle said. "I called you as soon as I finished. The whole thing is strange. I thought I better run it by you because you might want to run it by Armstrong before we do anything."

Riddle was referring to Mike Armstrong, the interim district attorney general who served four counties in Northeast Tennessee: Washington, Carter, Unicoi and Johnson.

"What's so strange about it?" Starring said.

"Might be a gang rape, might be a complete fabrication. There might be race involved, at least one black guy on a white woman. And if what this woman is saying is true, it happened at a party thrown by the ETSU football players last night, which is going to bring a lot of attention. The players hired a stripper, and she claims at least three guys pulled her into a bathroom and raped her. But there are some serious problems."

"Such as?" Starring said as he sipped his coffee.

"She says she was drugged and remembers very little about it, and her tox screen bears that out. She had a mixture of alcohol and ecstasy in her system, but the tox screen doesn't detect date rape drugs, and I think maybe some GHB or Rohypnol might be involved. She said somebody gave her a drink at the party and that's when she blacked out, so the drink may have had one of those drugs in it."

"Did we get a blood draw for a DFSA panel?" the chief asked.

"Actually, Officer James was on top of it. She woke up Judge Tinker and got an order. It's on its way to the lab. But she might have put the drug in the drink herself. She might be faking the whole thing. Who knows? The biggest problem is that she can't positively identify her attackers, although she thinks she remembers a black hand pulling her into the bathroom. She has a history of serious sexual abuse, which means she most likely has some psychological problems. She's on probation for heroin possession and she has two young children, both of whom were with her cousin last night while she was out stripping. She said she had sex with her boyfriend before she went to the party. She didn't call anybody after she left the party because she says she was too intoxicated. In fact, she didn't mention she was raped to anyone until she got picked up around 1:00 a.m. for refusing to leave a convenience store and found out she was going to Woodlawn for a mental evaluation."

"What did they say at the hospital?" Starring asked.

"That there were signs of sexual abuse. That it was within the realm of possibility that she was raped. Swollen vagina, a couple of bruises, but not serious bruises. They collected sperm samples and hair and did scrapings, the whole ball of wax."

Starring shook his head and stared down into his coffee.

"You're right, this could be a powder keg," he said. "Football players, strippers, race, the university. Damn, Riddle, it's Sunday morning. This is supposed to be my quiet time."

"You have to dump this on Armstrong," Riddle said. "He's the politician. He'll either think he can get something out of it or he won't, and that's how he'll make his decision. Won't have anything to do with the girl. She'll either be a pawn or a throwaway."

"That's a terribly cynical view of the criminal justice system, Investigator Riddle."

"It's what happens when you mix politics and criminal justice," Riddle said. "So… are you going to pack this off on Armstrong or make the call yourself?" Riddle said.

"Oh, I'm going to pack it off on Armstrong, no question. I said you were cynical. I didn't say you were wrong. I'm going to call Armstrong right now. I'll probably wind up going over to his house, and you're coming with me."

SUNDAY, AUGUST 25

District Attorney General Mike Armstrong opened his front door and said, "This better be important. I don't like to miss church."

"I'm sorry," Police Chief Gene Starring said. "I wouldn't have called you if it wasn't important. In fact, I think I'd call this one a little more than important. It could be explosive, Mike. You're going to have to make a tough decision."

The two men, along with Investigator Bo Riddle, walked into Armstrong's modestly decorated den inside his home in one of the older neighborhoods in North Johnson City. His wife had gone on to church, and his two girls had just gone back to Knoxville, where they were in college at the University of Tennessee, a hundred miles to the southwest.

"Sounds ominous," Armstrong said. "And ominous isn't good right now. There's an election next year. The primary is in April and only one person has made any noise about running against me. I don't need something that could blow up in my face."

Starring looked at Riddle and said, "Tell him what you told me."

As Riddle spoke, Starring watched Armstrong closely. Starring knew Armstrong was a lifelong prosecutor. He was roughly Starring's age – maybe a few years older – but unlike Starring, Armstrong looked his age. His hair was thick and snow white, and he was grossly underweight. Starring would have guessed his height at five feet, ten inches, and his weight at about a buck thirty. There was a large, brown mole in the middle of his forehead that Starring had to force himself to ignore.

Armstrong had come to Johnson City from Michigan only three years earlier because Armstrong's wife's mother, who had been a professor at the Bill Gatton College of Pharmacy at ETSU for five years during the school's infancy, had developed Alzheimer's disease and was in a long-term health care facility in Johnson City. Armstrong's father-in-law had left his wife fifteen years earlier for a much younger woman, and his mother-in-law had never remarried. Armstrong had told Starring when they first met that he'd never cared for his mother-in-law and didn't want to make the move, but his wife had made him feel so guilty that he'd eventually given in to her wishes and moved to Tennessee.

Because of Armstrong's experience, the prior district attorney, Tanner Jarrett, had hired him and immediately placed him in Criminal Court prosecuting felony cases, many of them serious, violent cases, and from everything Starring had heard, Armstrong was a competent prosecutor. Nothing spectacular, but competent. He didn't try a lot of cases, which wasn't out of the ordinary. About ninety percent of criminal cases were resolved through plea bargains. But when he did try a case, Armstrong

was, from everything Starring had heard, a good sales-
man. He related well to juries and got along with the
judges. Even the defense bar seemed to like him.

One thing that puzzled Starring, along with many
others in the law enforcement community, was how
Armstrong managed to get the interim district attorney general job in the first place. Tanner Jarrett, whose
wealthy father had served in the state senate and had
moved to Washington, D.C., had resigned six months
earlier and followed his father to the nation's capital.
He was now practicing law in one of D.C.'s prestigious
firms. Armstrong was outgoing and jovial, a glad-
hander who seemed to never have met a stranger, but
Northeast Tennesseans didn't usually trust outsiders,
especially outsiders from the north who talked with
hard, Midwestern accents.

Nonetheless, Armstrong had somehow managed to
get three of the most influential members of the county
commission to start lobbying the other members on
Armstrong's behalf, and within a month of Jarrett leaving, the county commission voted to appoint Armstrong
to finish out Tanner Jarrett's term. The move hadn't sat
well with several people in the district attorney's office,
and it had angered a fair amount of law enforcement
officers as well, but Armstrong seemed not to notice. He
stepped into the office with a smile on his face, as though
he was meant to be there and had been there all of his life.

"So that's about it," Riddle was saying, "warts
and all."

"Just to summarize," Armstrong said, "just to make
sure I have my facts straight, we have a gang rape that

may or may not have occurred. We're not even sure where the *house* is yet, but that'll be easy enough once we talk to the escort service. We have black on white rape allegations coming from what I would describe as a victim who is iffy at best, totally unreliable at worst. We have evidence and information from the rape nurse and doctor who performed the exam that suggest a rape may have occurred. We have a rape kit that contains quite a bit of material, including semen. But the victim has a history of sexual abuse, and she takes drugs. Not only is she not pristine, she had ecstasy and alcohol in her system, and maybe gamma hydroxybutyrate or Rohypnol. Plus she's been a stripper and a hooker for about three years. Am I doing okay so far?"

Both Riddle and Starring nodded their heads.

"So the question is whether we launch an investigation that will rock this town or tell this girl that because of the circumstances – her past, the drugs and alcohol, the fact that she can't remember anything and didn't report it as soon as she got out of there, the fact that she can't identify her attackers – that we would be hard pressed to get a conviction if we moved forward."

"That's what I recommend," Starring said. "Just for the record. I think we should tell her we're sorry, but there just isn't any way to make this stick."

"What if the semen inside of her comes back and contains DNA from one or more of those players?" Armstrong said.

"They'll say it was consensual," Starring said. "Like Bo said, she's a stripper and a hooker. It isn't too far-fetched to think that if they did have sex with her, it was because they slipped her a few more bucks. That's what the defense will say. Besides, they'd have to be fools to have sex with her without using a condom. From what Investigator Riddle says about this girl, the chances of them getting an STD would be about a hundred percent. My guess is there won't be any semen from a football player."

"I'll draft a search warrant application myself tomorrow," Armstrong said. "In the meantime, you guys find out where the house is and get all the information you can from the escort service. Tuesday morning, take your forensics people and your warrant and haul whoever you can in and interrogate them. I take allegations of rape very seriously. Not only that, if word of this gets out and people find out we had an allegation of a gang rape at a football party and sat on our hands or swept it under the rug, we'll get crucified. College football programs all over the country are getting a lot of attention when it comes to rape and sexual abuse. Did you see what happened at Baylor? Hell, they fired Ken Starr for goodness sakes. Do you remember Ken Starr?"

Starring had heard the name but couldn't place it.

"He was the special prosecutor that dogged Bill Clinton for years," Armstrong said. "After he quit prosecuting, he became the president at Baylor. There were several allegations of sexual abuse against football players, and the powers that be down there in Texas said Starr wasn't 'sensitive' enough to previous allegations and sent him packing. The coach and the athletic director went along with him."

"I still don't think it's a good idea," Starring said. "It's just a rotten case. I mean, this victim is not someone I want to get out in front of."

"Your reservations are noted," Armstrong said. "That's why you're here, to put the decision on me. All it would take would be one call from the rape nurse or the doc at the hospital or somebody from the escort service or even the girl herself. One call to the newspaper or a TV station, and all hell breaks loose. All hell is going to break loose anyway, so let's get in front of it and stay in front of it. We do it by the book."

"You're the boss," Starring said. "Get us a search warrant and we're on it. Are you going to call the TBI?"

"Not yet," Armstrong said. "Let's wait and see what you guys come up with."

TUESDAY, AUGUST 27

nvestigator Riddle looked at the monitor on the desk. It showed a strapping, handsome, young black man sitting in the wood-paneled interview room. He was wearing a gold East Tennessee State University football T-shirt. His hair was clipped closely to his scalp. His chin was resting on his hands. He didn't appear nervous, he didn't appear to be frightened. He was just sitting there, almost uninterested, as though being picked up for questioning in a gang rape was a part of his every day routine.

Riddle's blood pressure was up more than a little. He could feel his heart pumping and his fingers were trembling just a bit. He thought about walking in the room and getting a confession, no matter what it took. The chief was gone – he'd conveniently left for one of the many schools he attended each year – and Riddle was feeling like a stallion who'd just been unbridled. God, how he would love to get this kid to confess.

Riddle had hated jocks since junior high when he was cut from the football team because the coach said he just didn't have the mental and physical toughness required of a football player, and the guy in the interview room was ETSU's quarterback. Riddle hated ETSU because they'd fired his father, who'd worked on their maintenance staff for twenty years, for insubordination and repeated tardiness. And finally, he had no love for black people. Riddle was an unapologetic racist. He didn't wear it on his sleeve because he wanted to keep his job, but he came from a long line of racists who had taught him that black people didn't belong in America; they belonged in Africa. They'd been brought here involuntarily, forced into slavery, finally freed at a tremendous cost of white lives, and now they were angry, intolerant, and entitled. Riddle had been taught, and still sincerely believed, that black people thought the United States owed them because of what had happened hundreds of years ago. As far as Riddle's grandfathers, uncles and father were concerned, every black person in the U.S., male, female or mixed, should be shipped out to the African continent, and Riddle agreed with them. Riddle didn't care what country the deported blacks wound up in, as long as it wasn't his.

His work as a police officer had done nothing to change his attitude towards race. He'd arrested dozens of young black men for selling drugs, for domestic assaults, for robberies and for homicides. He'd dealt with the Crips and the Bloods and their seemingly endless game of senseless violence. He'd dealt with crackhead mothers who bore children by several different men and then dumped them onto grandparents – usually grandmothers – who had neither the means nor the desire to care for them. He'd seen the worst kind of behavior from them, and although he'd seen the same from whites, he just didn't stomach the behavior the same when it came to blacks. He perceived them as defiant, unrepentant and ignorant.

The kid in the room was named Kevin Davidson. Riddle knew virtually nothing about him other than he was a senior at ETSU, twenty-one-years old, had a Collierville address on his driver's license, and had no criminal record of any kind. But Riddle had convinced himself that this kid had raped a woman three days earlier. A white woman.

Riddle went into the bathroom and slapped himself in the face a couple of times, just to get his blood boiling a little more. As he washed his hands, he looked into the mirror at his shaved head and angry, chocolate brown eyes. His second wife had left him three months earlier and he'd put on fifteen pounds, most of it from sitting at home alone and drinking vodka when he was off work. The lines in his forehead had grown deeper and his skin had an ashy tone.

"You need to start working out again, fat ass," he said out loud to himself.

They'd executed the search warrant at 6:00 a.m. sharp at a house on Pine Street near the ETSU campus. The house was owned by ETSU and was occupied by three players, all seniors and all captains on the football team. Kevin Davidson was the only one of them who was awake when Riddle and the other officers arrived. He opened the door and seemed genuinely surprised to see the police. Riddle noticed some books and papers and an open laptop on a table in Kevin's room. It appeared he'd been studying before the police showed up. All three of the players had been cooperative and had agreed to ride to the police station to be questioned.

Riddle walked out of the bathroom and over to his partner, who was standing next to his desk waiting to go into the interview room. His partner was gangly and twenty-six years old, a virtual baby in police work, named Bret Marshall. Marshall had only been in the Criminal Investigation Division for two months.

"Let me do the talking," Riddle said.

"You got it."

"We're not recording this, so if I wind up thumping on him, you didn't see a thing."

"Absolutely."

"You have no problem with that?"

"I'm not crazy about it, but I guess you do what you have to do."

"That's right. If it gets to be too much for you, you can always leave the room. Let's go."

Riddle burst through the door and slammed a thin file down on the table. He turned a chair around backwards and moved to within two feet of Kevin Davidson.

"There's a theory in police work, Kevin, that the best way to conduct an interview is to coddle the suspect, make friends with him, gain his trust, and make him believe you're there to help him. It's all a lie, of course. So I'm going to tell you right off the top, I'm not here to help you. Do you understand that?"

"Yes, sir, but I don't understand why I'm here."

"See? Now that kind of thing right there pisses me off and could wind up getting you hurt. I know how to hurt suspects, Kevin. I can beat them within an inch of their lives and not put a bruise on them. People lying to me pisses me off, and me getting pissed off causes me to beat on people sometimes."

"So you're telling me you're going to beat me?"

The young man's eyebrows raised, but he still didn't seem frightened.

"That depends on whether you tell me the truth."

"Maybe I should get a lawyer," Kevin said. "I don't think I like the way this is going."

"Why would you want a lawyer? Have you done something wrong?"

"No."

"Then why would you want a lawyer?"

"Because you just threatened to beat me."

"Nah, nah, you misunderstood me, Kevin. I said you wouldn't get beaten if you told the truth. Isn't that what I said, Investigator Marshall?"

"That's exactly what you said."

"You already signed your Miranda waiver," Riddle said. "That means you agreed to talk to us and waived your right to have an attorney present."

"I can change my mind," Kevin said.

Riddle laughed and looked at Marshall. "He can change his mind. Did you hear that? He thinks he's a lawyer."

"I'm not an idiot," Kevin said. "I've studied it in school. I'm a criminal justice major, and I have a 4.2 Grade Point Average. I've already been accepted to law school. I have a right to remain silent, no matter what."

"Well, whoop-dee-doo for Kevin with the big brain," Riddle said. "What say we stop all this tap dancing and get down to it? Tell me about the party."

"Saturday night? Is that what this is about?"

Kevin and his two roommates – Dominic Vasso and Henry Treadway – were being interrogated at the same time. Six investigators – which was all the Criminal Investigation Division had, along with a captain – were interviewing suspects in three separate rooms. Depending upon how the initial interviews went, the Tennessee Bureau of Investigation was standing by waiting to help.

"You tell me," Riddle said. "What happened?"

"Nothing happened. It was the week before the season started, we'd been busting our tails, and we figured we'd blow off some steam and have a party. One of the guys mentioned hiring a stripper. It started out as a joke, but it just sort of took on a life of its own. Thinking back on it now, was it a great idea? No. It was a terrible idea. But we did it and I can't undo it. When the girl got there, this pretty redhead, she came up to me and chatted for a few seconds. She got her cash from one of the other guys and then she disappeared for a little while, and when she came back, she was stumbling all over the place. She must have taken something, because she was really messed up. She eventually started trying to do her thing, but she was so out of it she wound up just falling on the floor. Some guys got pissed off and started saying they wanted their money back. There was some name-calling, and eventually the girl made her way out the front door. Another argument started and she wound up staggering up the street. She left. That was it."

"What was the argument about outside?"

"Same stuff as inside. Guys wanted their money back. She tossed out some racial stuff."

"Did it get physical?"

"No. Did anybody call the cops? Because no cops showed up until you guys came this morning. Which is kind of strange, don't you think?"

"Being a wise ass will get you hurt," Riddle said. "Who hired her?"

"One of my teammates."

"Which one?" Riddle said.

"I'm not ratting out a teammate. What difference does it make, anyway?"

"Tell me which teammate paid her."

"No."

"You're obstructing justice."

"Then charge me."

"You're pissing me off, boy. How much was she paid?"

"Three hundred, *boy*. Plus we were supposed to tip her."

Riddle could feel himself about to blow. Did this nigger just call him boy? He wanted to smash the quarterback's face in.

"Where do you get three hundred bucks for a stripper plus money for a tip? You slinging dope on the side?"

"I'm not selling drugs, and neither is anybody else at our house. You won't find anything in our house and you can test me for drugs if you want. The money was pooled from the guys. There are eighty guys on our team including the redshirts. Some of them ponied five bucks, a couple of them threw in thirty."

"What about you, Mr. Quarterback? How much did you throw in the pot?"

"Twenty. I put twenty dollars in."

"Do you know the penalty in Tennessee for kidnapping and rape?"

"What? Kidnapping and rape? Nobody got kidnapped because she showed up by herself and left when she wanted. Nobody held her against her will. And nobody got raped."

"That's not what the girl says."

"The stripper? She says she was raped?"

"She was pulled into the bathroom and raped by three guys. One of them was black, she says, and a captain."

"She's lying. And just for your information, there are two black captains, two white captains, and a Mexican captain on our team. And I want a lawyer."

"You waived your right to a lawyer."

"I'm not saying another word to you. Arrest me right now or let me go."

Suddenly, Riddle threw his chair to the side, grabbed Kevin by the shirt and threw him up against the wall. Kevin was taller, leaner and probably stronger than Riddle, but Riddle was thick and had obviously done this kind of thing before. He shoved his forearm under Kevin's chin.

"You worthless ni…"

"Worthless what?" Kevin said. "Nigger? Were you about to call me a worthless nigger? Go ahead. And you want to beat on me? Go ahead. I've taken worse than you can dish out. Besides, I'm not NFL material. I'm going to law school so I can sue gorilla cops like you that think with their balls because they don't have brains. So go ahead and beat me. I can use the extra money I'll make suing the city and you, pork chop."

Riddle could feel his eyes bulging. He wanted to crush this wise ass's windpipe. Instead, he kneed Kevin in the testicles and stood back as Kevin melted to the floor, retching.

"You're going to the penitentiary for kidnapping and rape," Riddle said. "I'm gonna see to it personally. I'll be so far up your ass you'll feel me tickling your throat."

Riddle walked to the door and looked down at Kevin, who was still gagging on the floor.

"You're free to go for now," Riddle said. "You can crawl out the same way you walked in."

TUESDAY, AUGUST 27

Captain Trent Bingham looked around the small conference room at the faces of his six investigators. They were all seated, all fidgeting. Some were fiddling with their phones. Some were looking at the ceiling. The mood was somber. Only Bo Riddle was staring at him. From everything Bingham had heard so far, it had been an unproductive morning.

"Did anybody get anything we can use?" the captain said.

"The black kid is lying," Investigator Riddle said. "He's dirty on this."

"Did he confess? Did he make any statements at all that implicated him in a rape?"

"The girl says one of the guys that raped her was black," Riddle said.

"How many black guys are on the team?" Bingham said.

"I don't know," Riddle said.

"I'm looking at a photo of the team on their website," said an investigator in the back. "It looks like there are forty-six black guys on the team."

"Great. Where'd the money to pay the strippers come from?"

"He said they took up a collection from the team," Riddle said.

"The girl's story is full of holes," Bingham said. "You guys know it and I know it. Riddle, what makes you think he's guilty?"

"I just don't like him. He's smug. He thinks he's going to get away with this."

"You don't like anybody. Does anybody else have anything?"

The rest of the detectives looked at each other with blank faces.

"So nobody is willing to roll on anybody?"

"Our guy said nothing happened. Just an argument and the girl left," Investigator David Morgan said.

"Same with ours," Investigator Benny Garrett said. "He says she's flat out lying. She showed up, then disappeared for a few minutes, and when she came back she was too intoxicated to perform. Said she could barely stand up. He said there are cell phone videos that will back him up."

"Great," Bingham said, "Another thing I'd like to know is whether anybody in this room leaked this to the press. I got a call from a reporter at the Johnson City paper a half-hour ago."

There was silence.

"I suppose quite a few people know about it by now, but I swear to God if I find out one of you guys is talking to the press about an ongoing investigation, I'll have your badge."

"So what do we do?" Riddle said.

Bingham looked at his most seasoned investigator. Riddle's cheeks were flushed, which meant he was angry. Bingham had known Riddle was a hot head for years. He might even have been a racist, but if he was, he hid it well. He hadn't been caught stepping over any lines, hadn't done anything that would allow Chief Starring to get rid of him. There had been a couple of excessive force complaints, but those were routine and usually were resolved when a camera revealed – or a fellow officer gave a statement – that a suspect was resisting.

"This could blow up in our faces," Bingham said, "so everything is by the book. We let Chief Starring and the district attorney handle the press. We let the lab people do their thing. I want every one of you back over there in that neighborhood and I want it canvassed. I'm going to call the football coach myself and find out how many players are willing to talk to us. If something happened, somebody will speak up."

"And if they don't?" Riddle said.

"Then maybe nothing happened. Maybe it was just a bunch of testosterone-filled young men who hired a stripper and things didn't go as planned. Keep in mind we're in the business of proving cases, not manufacturing them. That's it. Let's get to it."

WEDNESDAY, AUGUST 28

A s had been my habit for years, I walked barefoot up the driveway wearing only my boxer shorts and pulled the newspaper out of the box. It was 5:15 a.m., still dark, and our German shepherd, Rio, and our teacup poodle, Chico, had veered off into the yard to relieve themselves. Caroline was sound asleep in the bedroom. The slight breeze out of the west was warm. It promised to be a hot, humid day in Northeast Tennessee.

I walked back down the driveway, through the garage, and into the kitchen. The dogs went back to the bedroom to stretch out and get some more sleep while I dropped the paper on the table and poured myself a cup of coffee. I walked back over to the table, sat down, and did a double-take at the headline above the fold of the Johnson City paper: "Football Players Allegedly Rape Stripper at Party."

"Wow," I said as I began to read. The story was lurid and shocking, but as I read through it a couple of times, the lawyer in me began to realize that the story was also full of what could turn out to be unsubstantiated accusations. If the facts alleged in the story were true, there would be dire consequences for East Tennessee State

University and its football program, which had only been re-established two years earlier after being disbanded for ten years due to tight budget conditions and general lack of fan interest at the state-funded institution. But there were things about the story that bothered me, not the least of which was that the stripper who reported the rape supposedly didn't do so until hours after the rape, and it took the police almost three days to execute a search warrant on the home where the party took place. The three players who lived at the home were there when the police arrived, according to the story, and they gave statements and even helped the police search the house.

Basically, what the story said was that a group of more than sixty players had held a party at an off-campus house that was owned by the university and occupied by three senior captains of the football team. The three seniors weren't named in the story, nor were any of the other players, but it said football players were the only people in attendance. I found that hard to believe. Who can keep a lid on a college party where a stripper will be performing? The party was held on a Saturday night, a week before the season was supposed to begin. According to the story, the police were alleging – which meant the stripper was alleging – that three unidentified members of the football team had dragged her into a small bathroom and raped her over a period of about twenty minutes. When the stripper was finally allowed to leave the bathroom, everyone else had left the party. It was the kind of journalism I'd grown to hate over the years, but it was becoming more and more prevalent. No sources were quoted directly, citing either an ongoing investigation or the privacy rights of college students. Unsubstantiated allegations were presented as though they were fact. It was as though the newspaper reporters (two of them contributed, one male and one female) were trying to incite something rather than simply report the news.

I was sitting there fuming over the incompetence of the journalists when I heard Caroline plodding toward the kitchen.

"How can you stand to be up so early in the morning?" she mumbled as she went to the refrigerator and poured herself a glass of orange juice. I knew it was time for her pain medication that she took for the cancer in her bones.

"How can you stand to be in bed so late?" I said.

"It's easy," she said. "Whenever I think about getting up, I just close my eyes and go back to sleep. Is there anything in the fish wrapper this morning?"

Caroline didn't care much for the Johnson City paper. The old ownership had sold out to a large conglomerate and they'd fired more than half the staff, some of whom Caroline and I had known for years.

"There's actually a sensational, front-page story about football players and a stripper at a party," I said. "There may or may not have been a rape. Maybe even a gang rape."

Her eyebrows lifted as she lowered the glass of orange juice and took a couple of steps toward me.

"Anything to it?" she said.

"Hard to tell. A bunch of anonymous sources and unconfirmed information."

"Oh, you mean standard operating procedure for journalism these days."

I shrugged my shoulders.

"Who knows?" I said. "It might be nothing or it might be a serious crime."

"Sounds to me like people might be needing lawyers," she said.

"I don't do sex cases, Caroline. You know that."

I hadn't had a nightmare about my sister, Sarah, being raped by my sixteen-year-old uncle when we were very young since Caroline and I had talked about it in the car on the way home from Vanderbilt a few days earlier. The incident had had a profound impact on both Sarah and me, because I'd tried unsuccessfully to stop him and because Sarah had had to endure the terrible humiliation of the rape at such a young age. When I started practicing defense law, I vowed I would never defend a rapist.

"But you now practice law with your son, Jack Dillard, and a young woman named Charlie Story, who just happens to be his girlfriend and who I predict he will marry sometime within the next year. I know your reasons for not taking sex cases. Will your associates be barred from taking cases because you refuse to do so?"

"There may not even be a case, Caroline."

"But if there is, will you keep Jack and Charlie from taking on a rape case because your sister was raped when she was a child? That doesn't seem quite fair to me."

"Wow, you must be feeling pretty good this morning. You've come out of the bedroom with both guns blazing. Has anyone even tried to hire us? If so, I'm unaware."

"Just think about it," Caroline said as she turned away. "Jack and Charlie share your law practice now. They also share your passion and your talent. But they don't share your past, and they shouldn't be burdened by it. If someone is accused of committing a rape in that house, needs a good lawyer, and wants to hire you, you should give some serious consideration to taking it on and letting them help you."

WEDNESDAY, AUGUST 28

The president of East Tennessee State University was as angry as he'd ever been in his life when his football coach walked through the door of his expansive, tastefully-appointed office at 8:00 a.m. the morning the story broke about the rape allegations against football players. Already in the room were the university's general counsel, the director of community relations, and the athletic director.

The president, a forty-six-year-old named Dean Brady, had been employed by the university for five years. During his tenure, he'd worked hard to engage the university with the community, he'd worked hard to improve programs in the arts, in academics and in athletics. He'd spearheaded the movement to return football to the university after the program had been shut down for ten years. Brady, who had never played football, nonetheless believed the sport to be an important part of the student experience on a college campus and an absolute necessity if the university was to improve itself and thrive in the future.

Brady had taken a great deal of criticism for his stance on football, especially from faculty members and administrators on the academic side who believed the sport to be a burden on an already strained budget. There were also a majority of students who didn't want the sport returned to campus and had made their feelings known through a vote. But in the end, it didn't matter. The powers that controlled the purse strings – and the ability to assess students' extra tuition to pay for the football program – ultimately prevailed and the sport returned. A veteran football coach named Mike Springer had been hired to build the program. During their first season, where they played on a local high school field because they didn't have a stadium, they posted a predictable but abysmal record of 2-9. The following year, still playing at the high school, they improved to 5-6. This year was to be the true beginning. A new stadium had been built on campus. The players were experienced and the team had become stronger in every phase of the game. Springer had been quoted as saying he believed his team could win at least seven games.

There was a long silence after Coach Springer took his seat at the round table in the corner across the office from Brady's desk. The president had a copy of the Johnson City newspaper spread out in front of him. He finally looked at Springer and said, "What in the hell are we going to do about this?"

"I don't believe she was raped," Coach Springer said. "I just don't see my guys doing something like that."

"Did you envision your guys hiring a stripper for a party?" Brady said. "Did you know anything about it?"

"Of course not," Springer said.

"Have you talked to any of them yet?"

"I talked to the three captains who live in the house where the party was held. They all say nothing happened, and I believe them. The stripper idea started as a joke and then turned into a real thing, but again, I don't believe for a second that a rape took place. I plan to talk to every player on the team. I'll get to the bottom of this."

"We need to respond to this as quickly as possible," said Blakely Burton, the director of community relations for the university. She was a blonde former television news anchor who was now the university's mouthpiece and drafted or approved nearly all official communications that went from the university to any news outlet. "There needs to be a statement from you, Dr. Brady. What we have to decide is whether we announce that we're going to be proactive and what kind of action we plan to take or whether we plan to refrain from comment, rely on the laws that protect students' privacy, and allow the police investigation to run its course. We can take appropriate action accordingly. That would be my recommendation. A statement that basically says nothing."

"We have a problem besides just the police investigation," the president said. "I spoke to the chief of police an hour ago. The young woman making the accusations is also a part-time student here, which means Title IX and all of its ramifications come into play."

He looked across the table at George Darden, the school's general counsel. Darden was in his late forties. His blond hair was thinning quickly and his eyes were a robin's egg shade of blue. He was an avid runner who competed in marathons and was, therefore, slightly built. He'd graduated from Yale law school and was a seasoned lawyer and a tough negotiator. Brady trusted him completely.

"George," the president said. "Why don't you bring them up to speed?"

"It's actually pretty tricky in this case," Darden said. "I'm sure everyone in this room knows that Title IX is a federal civil rights statute passed in 1972 to protect women from sexual discrimination on college campuses across the country. The fact that the woman making these accusations is a student here, added to the fact that the house where those three captains live is owned by the university, may obligate us to conduct our own investigation into the incident and eventually hold a hearing to see whether the players should be expelled for their conduct. If she doesn't file a formal complaint, however, then we may not be obligated. I'm just not sure. I know of no precedent where a stripper who was also a student at a university sued the university after being sexually assaulted by other students on property controlled by the university. They say there's nothing new under the sun, but this might be. Right now, she's gone to the authorities and they are apparently actively investigating this as a possible kidnapping and rape. If it happened, if she was really raped or sexually assaulted in any way, and the criminal justice system indicts them and tries them, we're going to get sued and we'll wind up paying through the nose. The girl will allege we didn't protect her. She'll probably sue us even if there is no criminal prosecution. So again, it goes back to you, Coach, as far as the institution is concerned. Did you or any of your assistant coaches know anything about this? *Should* you have known? If you didn't know, then why not? The ultimate question will be: 'Just what kind of program are you running?'"

"And I'll be the scapegoat," Coach Springer said.

"It might come down to that, but you might not be alone," Darden said. He turned his attention to Raymond Winters, the university's athletic director.

"Is there anything we should know, Raymond?"

Winters, who was nearing sixty and had been the director of athletics for fifteen years, raised his eyebrows.

"Like what?"

"Have there been Title IX accusations of sexual assault against athletes that you haven't told us about? Anything swept under the rug? Because it's becoming a thing right now for plaintiffs' lawyers to go after universities because universities aren't good at dealing with sexual assaults, especially when it comes to athletes. Baylor's football program got crushed. The president, the athletic director, the head football coach and nearly the entire football staff were sent packing. They'll pay out tens of millions before it's over. The University of Tennessee just paid out three million to eight plaintiffs. It's happening all over the country. If we get hammered with a big payout, the Board of Trustees will disband the football team again and it won't be back."

"We can't hire lawyers for these guys, can we?" Coach Springer said.

"No. And if some alumni or booster tries to go around the rules and starts hiring lawyers, again, football will be gone."

"I got a call from a police captain," the coach said. "He wants to know whether all of my guys will voluntarily give DNA samples and come in for interviews. The three players that were in the house, Kevin Davidson, Dominic Vasso and Henry Treadway, already talked to them and gave them DNA samples. I told him I'd have to talk to you about it first, George. What do you think?"

"My first instinct is to tell them no," Darden said. "I wouldn't want to give them the opportunity to manipulate evidence the way that fool prosecutor did at Duke University ten years ago. Besides, they have the right to remain silent and that's always a good policy when you might be a suspect in a crime. If the DA gets subpoenas from a judge for DNA samples from every player, we can fight it. If we lose, we lose, but at least we'll look like we're backing our players."

"I disagree," Dr. Brady said. "Blakely, you write up a release for the press and I'll go over it," President Brady said. "Make it as noncommittal as possible. Raymond, I want you back in here by noon to give me a report on Title IX cases and how they've been handled. Don't write anything down. And Coach Springer, you go to your guys and tell them I said thanks a hell of a lot. With one act of stupidity, rape or no rape, they've tarnished the reputation of this university and have endangered everything we've worked so hard to build. I also want you to tell them to cooperate fully with the police. Interviews, DNA samples, whatever they need."

"I just don't think that's in their best interests," Darden said.

"I don't give a damn about their best interest right now," Brady said. "I care about this university and what it means to this community. If one or more of those guys is a rapist, then I want their scalps hanging from the upper deck of the football stadium. Everybody cooperates with the police. Let's do anything and everything to get this out of the news and behind us as quickly as we possibly can. And George?"

"Yes, Dr. Brady?"

"Start checking into whether we can pay this woman off. I want to know how much it'll take to make her go away."

THURSDAY, AUGUST 29

Caroline turned out to be a prophet, because the call came in later that day. Gerome Davidson, an assistant city manager in Collierville, wanted to meet with me along with his wife, Regina, and his son, Kevin. The call came into the office in Jonesborough, where Charlie and Jack and I had updated things. We'd expanded into a rental space that had become vacant next door, so we now had offices for me, for Jack, and for Charlie. We also had a decent-sized conference room and small offices for our new legal secretary and a paralegal.

The secretary was a sharp, mid-thirties blonde named Beverly Snyder and the paralegal was a younger, equally-sharp brunette named Kelly Sims, both of whom had been hired by Jack and Charlie. I'd had a secretary years earlier, but Caroline had become my secretary when I decided to get out of practicing criminal defense law. That only lasted a couple of years. When I went back to criminal defense, Caroline handled the secretarial duties, but she didn't much care for it and she no longer had the energy. We also had a new investigator, a former FBI agent who had retired after twenty years with the bureau and was hiring herself out as a private investigator on a case-by-case basis. Her name was Susan Stoneman, but everybody called her Stony. She'd worked two cases for us, and I'd found her work to be excellent and her rates reasonable.

So we'd hired the new people, had the new office set up, and had updated all of our computers and software. We were capable of being a regular legal defense juggernaut now, a real team with good people and the right technology. Because of all the changes, and especially because I had Jack and Charlie around all the time, I'd found myself revitalized when it came to practicing law. I was often lost when it came to using the tech stuff, but I was enjoying the practice of law for the first time in a long time.

Charlie was in court when the call came in from Gerome Davidson and I was at the jail talking to an appointed client named Rocky Rutledge who had been accused of murdering his brother-in-law, so Beverly initially turned the call over to Jack. Jack spoke with Mr. Davidson for quite some time and set up an appointment for the next day. Mr. Davidson, who had driven up from Collierville as soon as his son told him what was going on, wanted me there. He said he'd done some calling around and believed I would be the best person for the job, so Jack told him, without talking to me, that I'd be there. I was a bit annoyed at first, but after thinking about what Caroline had said and after listening to what Jack had to say, I agreed.

The three of them walked in at 11:00 a.m. sharp, right on time. Beverly buzzed me and told me they were there. By the time I walked out into the lobby, she'd offered them coffee or tea or water, which they all turned down. I greeted each of them separately.

Kevin was an impressive looking young man. He was about two inches shorter than me at six-feet-one, and he was lean and muscular. He had a firm handshake and he looked me directly in the eye when I took his hand. He had beautiful, perfect white teeth, short hair, high cheekbones and a long face. Everything about him said athlete, the way he looked, the way he moved. He was wearing a charcoal gray suit and tie over a white button-down shirt.

His parents were a handsome couple as well. Kevin was practically a clone of Gerome, while Regina was striking in a navy-blue business suit. She wore her hair short, and was as lean as the men in her life. She would later tell me that she ran track at Middle Tennessee State University, where she was a 400 and 800-meter specialist and where she had met her husband, who was a linebacker on the football team majoring in public administration.

I brought the three of them into my office and we made some small talk. Gerome and Regina had been married right out of college and Kevin came along the very next year. He was now twenty-one years old, which meant they'd been married for twenty-two. They also had two daughters, both of whom were in high school in Collierville. Kevin had been an all-state performer at Collierville. He'd drawn the attention of some Division I programs, but none of them wanted him to play quarterback. He was left-handed and said while his arm was plenty strong, he wasn't consistently accurate. He could run, though, and he eventually wound up at East Mississippi Community College in a small town called Scooba, Mississippi. He played very little there, didn't like the coach, and transferred to ETSU after being invited to visit. The Bucs were a Division I FCS school just putting a program back together. They didn't even have a stadium in which to play during Kevin's first two years but were scheduled to move into a brand-new stadium on campus his senior season. The team won two games Kevin's first year, had won five games last year, and were hoping to win at least seven this year. The young man's eyes lit up when he talked about football; I could tell he loved it.

"And what kind of student are you?" I asked.

"Top of my class," he said. "Majoring in criminal justice and minoring in history. I've already been accepted to law school at the University of Tennessee. I guess that could change, depending on what happens in this case."

"I went to the University of Tennessee law school," I said. "Good school, but I barely remember it. I was married, we were having and raising babies. I was so busy it's just a blur."

"I hope Kevin gets the opportunity to go there," his father said. "He's worked hard, and up until the other night, has made good decisions for the most part."

"Right. Okay, let's talk about the other night," I said. "And Kevin, I'm just going to be honest with you. I don't want to take this case. Someone close to me was raped when she was very young, and I know how devastating something like that can be. Usually, when criminal defense lawyers talk to clients, especially for the first time, they kind of dance around the facts of the case. The lawyer isn't necessarily looking to find out if his client is innocent, because more than ninety percent of the time the client is guilty. So the lawyer looks for ways to attack the prosecution's case by trying to find things the police may have done incorrectly. We look for constitutional violations, anything that can get our client out of the charge, or at the very least, put us in a better plea-bargaining position. But with you, I'm not going to do that. You're going to have to convince me you're innocent or I'm not going to take this case. I'm not going to represent a rapist, plain and simple. If you can't convince me during this meeting that you didn't commit this rape, you'll have to find somebody else."

"There was no rape," Kevin said. "Nothing happened. You're not going to kick me in the testicles, are you?"

"What? Why would you say that?"

"Because that's what the cop did. I wouldn't tell him what he wanted to hear so he kicked me in the testicles. I nearly passed out."

That pissed me off immediately. I hated police brutality almost as much as I hated rapists.

"Who was the cop?"

"Skinhead named Riddle."

Bo Riddle. I knew him well, or at least I'd known him professionally for a long time. I'd always suspected him of being a racist and had heard stories of him beating on suspects, but I'd never been able to pin anything on him. I made a mental note to make sure that changed in the near future.

"Okay, if I take this, I'll deal with Riddle," I said. "I promise you I'll deal with him for assaulting you. But before we go there, what did you tell him?"

"I told him we hired a stripper, which we did. One of my buddies called the escort service. A couple of my friends got the money together from the players and put the party together. The girl showed up, she chatted some of the guys up, including me, for a few minutes, and then she said she was going into the bathroom to change and would start her show. When she came back out, she was too messed up to do anything. She could barely walk."

"Know her name?" I said.

"No. The paper isn't printing it and the cops didn't tell me. I called the escort service and asked them, but they hung up on me."

"Why in the hell did you hire a stripper to come to a party in the first place? I mean, even if this hadn't happened, didn't you think word would have gotten out?"

"Nothing happened," Kevin said. "And as far as why we did it, I really can't tell you. It wasn't my idea, but I didn't say no, either, when it came up. We'd been working our butts off, and we just felt like we needed to do something to loosen everybody up and have some fun before the season started."

"So objectifying and sexually exploiting women is your idea of fun?" I said.

He was silent for several seconds. Then he looked at me and said, "You don't like me much, do you?"

His parents were shifting in their seats. I don't think the meeting was going quite the way they expected it to go.

"I don't know you," I said. "But I have to tell you I don't tend to like people who objectify and exploit women. I have some wonderful women in my life that I love and respect, and I already told you about the rape incident, so when someone walks in here and says, 'We hired a stripper to dance at a football party,' it sticks in my craw a little."

"Before we continue," Gerome said, "may I ask you a personal question?"

I shrugged my shoulders. "Sure."

"Are you a racist?"

I figured the question might be coming, but I still found it a little disconcerting. Because I was vigorously questioning his son, I was a racist? What he didn't know was that over the years, while practicing criminal defense, I'd asked myself that question many times. The answer, to me, was far more complicated than a simple yes or no.

"I don't think so," I said to Gerome. "I don't think I'm a racist any more than you or anyone else. I think the better question, Mr. Davidson, is when I see a black man or a brown man or anyone of a different race, do I automatically hate that person? The answer to *that* question is an unqualified no. Do I judge them differently than I do white people? I don't think so. I certainly don't do it consciously. My mother was an uneducated Southern woman. She hated a lot of things, including the government as an institution, many individuals in government – especially those that had to do with our involvement in the Vietnam War – and she despised organized religion. But she didn't hate people based on their skin color, so I didn't have that ingrained into me from a parent or family member like so many racists do. I've represented black men and women and Latino men and women who have done some pretty horrible things, just like I've represented white men and women who have done horrible things. I look at them as flawed human beings, not as flawed black people or Latinos or white people. So I guess the simple answer to your question is no, I'm not a racist.

"Now ask me if I look at a black man or woman I don't know and automatically love them. The answer is no, I don't. Do I even trust them? To a certain degree, I suppose I do. I try to give people the benefit of the doubt, although I admit it's difficult after you've been in my profession for as long as I have. But I can't sit here and tell you that I love everyone, because I don't. That doesn't make me a racist, does it?

"What I *can* tell you is that race will become a part of this case if your son winds up being arrested and charged with sexually assaulting or raping or kidnapping a white woman, even if she was a stripper. Racism and hatred are as alive and well here in Northeast Tennessee as anywhere else. I'm sure you heard about the incident last year at the Black Lives Matter rally on the ETSU campus where the white kid showed up in a gorilla mask. He had bananas dangling from strings and a burlap sack with a confederate flag and a marijuana leaf on it. He was offering bananas to the black protestors. The police arrested him and charged him with civil rights intimidation, and he'll probably be convicted, but it'll be reversed on appeal. Was he trying to provoke them? Sure. Intimidate them to keep them from doing something? No. He probably had as much right to be there as they did, gorilla mask and all, under the first amendment. But because what he did probably wasn't illegal didn't make it right. He was an ignorant kid promoting hatred and bigotry. It's a shame. It really is.

"Let me give you one more example of what you'll be up against if Kevin gets charged and we wind up going to trial. I was trying a crack cocaine case a few years back. I was appointed to represent a black man with a couple of prior drug convictions who had done ten years in the penitentiary. He wasn't on parole – he'd flattened his sentence – but there was a drug task force agent in Johnson City who hated him and wanted him back in prison. My client's name was Freddie. Freddie didn't sell any crack cocaine the night he was arrested, and he didn't have any in his possession. He'd smoked some earlier in the night, but this cop didn't know that. What the cop did was get one of his scumbag informants to call Freddie and ask him to help the informant find a hundred-dollars-worth of crack. The drug agent paid his informant fifty dollars to make the call. My client, who had known the informant for a long time, agreed to help the guy find a few rocks. He took him to a park and pointed out a dealer. He wasn't involved in the transaction, didn't get any drugs. But Freddy facilitated it, so they charged him with conspiracy to sell and distribute. He was a multiple offender, so he was looking at twelve years. We walk into the courtroom for jury selection and I look around the room. Not a black face in the crowd. The black population in the county is only around three percent, and I guess the Criminal Court

Clerk just didn't bother making sure any black jurors got summoned for jury duty. We start questioning the potential jurors, and I tell them my client is scared. I tell them he's scared because he's the only black man in the courtroom. The judge absolutely went off on me. He's retired now, but he was an idiot. His name was Ivan Glass, and he made a speech about racism being a thing of the past, that Jim Crow was over and that the civil rights movement had done away with racism in the United States and that white people could judge black people without any bias whatsoever. I told him he was a fool and almost went to jail for contempt. But I have to tell you, that attitude is still prevalent with some of the judges. They don't think racism exists. They just don't get it."

"They're wrong," Gerome said. "It's getting worse by the day. What happened to Freddy?"

"The jury nullified. I showed them the rocks. They were tiny. The informant admitted he sought Freddie out and talked him into helping him find a dealer – it was all on tape. But Freddie didn't get anything out of the deal. Under a strict interpretation of the law, Freddy was guilty, but they found him not guilty and let him go. The judge gave me another speech afterward saying the verdict proved his point, but Freddy didn't walk because there weren't any racists on the jury. He walked because I was able to convince them how stupid and unfair the entire prosecution was. He should never have been arrested."

"Kevin made a mistake," Gerome said. "Hiring the stripper was a mistake. You have a son, Mr. Dillard, I talked with him on the phone yesterday. Has he ever made a mistake?"

I started to say something about Jack never having hired a stripper, but did I really know that? He'd played Division I baseball with a bunch of alpha males for years. He'd played in the minor leagues. He was an alpha himself. I was sure he hadn't told me everything he'd done while he was out on his own, and if I was truly honest with myself, I didn't want to know.

"I'm sure he's made mistakes," I said. "But I don't think he's done anything that could land him in the penitentiary for thirty or forty years."

I turned back to Kevin and said, "You haven't been charged yet, but I assume they took DNA from you, correct?"

Kevin nodded. "They had a warrant for DNA samples from me and the other two guys who live in the house. They swabbed the inside of our mouths first thing."

"If they find your DNA in her or on her, you're in for a difficult time."

"They won't find anything."

"Did you touch her?"

"No."

I noticed he had some pretty deep scratches on both of his arms.

"Where'd you get those?" I said.

"Practice. I have scratches and bruises on me all the time."

"Anything else you need to tell me?"

"I don't think so."

"Who paid the girl?"

"One of my roommates. We took up a collection from all the guys on the team that wanted to come to the party."

"You contribute?"

"Twenty bucks."

"Your fingerprints will be on some of the money, then, if the cops get their hands on it before it gets distributed or deposited in a bank account somewhere."

"What does that prove?"

"Nothing, just a little piece of circumstantial evidence. Maybe it won't come up. Did the cops say anything about having the money? Did they fingerprint you?"

"No."

"Then they don't have it. How many guys were at the party?"

"Probably sixty, seventy."

"Any girls besides the one you hired?"

"I noticed maybe ten girls."

"Know any of their names?"

"Yeah, I know a few of them."

"People taking pictures with their phones?"

"Yeah. Videos and photos."

"We'll need a list of everybody you can think of who was at the party. What has your coach had to say?"

"Besides the cussing we took? He said we've endangered everything we've worked for, everything he and the other coaches have worked for, and everything the university administration has worked for. He told us they intend to cooperate fully with the police to the extent that the rules of privacy will allow them, and he said if he finds out that a rape occurred, he hopes whoever did it rots in the penitentiary before rotting in hell."

"Doesn't beat around the bush, does he?"

"Coach is a good man."

"Had you had anything to drink that night, Kevin?"

"I don't drink, Mr. Dillard. Never have. I've never smoked pot, never done anything like that. I take care of my body and I like to have a clear head."

"Good," I said. "You're going to need it."

"Have I convinced you I'm innocent?" he said.

"You haven't done or said a thing that makes me think you'd kidnap and rape a stranger. I've been dealing with criminal defendants for more than two decades, and I'm a pretty good judge of when someone is trying to pull something over on me. I don't get that sense from you."

"So you'll represent me?"

I nodded.

"How much is this going to cost?" Gerome said.

"I don't know," I said. "It depends on what the DNA tests find and what the district attorney does. If Kevin winds up being prosecuted, it'll be expensive. Let's just wait and see how it goes. We'll deal with money when the time comes."

PART TWO

THURSDAY, AUGUST 29

Jack hollered at me a few minutes after the Davidsons left.

"Come to the conference room!" he said.

"Why?" I yelled back.

"Just come in here. You have to see this."

I walked out of my office and down the hall to the conference room. The television was on. Mike Armstrong, the interim district attorney general, was giving an interview to a Fox television reporter.

"Yes," Armstrong was saying, "in my opinion, a rape occurred at a party thrown by the East Tennessee State University football team. The young woman who was raped was an exotic dancer hired by the players. She claims she was raped by multiple players, and I have good reason to believe her."

"Have you identified suspects?"

"We've talked to the players who rent the house where the party took place. We've searched the house and taken DNA samples from those players at the house. We intend to take DNA samples from every player and interview as many of them as we can."

"And is the university and football program being cooperative?" the reporter, who was one of the network's better-known guys, asked.

"Not in my view. We haven't heard anything from anyone other than the players who were living in the house," Armstrong said.

I looked at Jack open-mouthed.

"What does he think he's doing?" I said. "He's giving interviews to the press on a case that hasn't gone to the grand jury? There hasn't even been an arrest and he's giving interviews?"

"He's talking to anybody and everybody," Jack said. "*The New York Times* has a story on their website. *Time* Magazine has mentioned it. He's talked to both of them. He's talking to the local papers and television stations. He's not only trying to convict them before they're arrested, he's poisoning potential jurors."

"It's unethical," I said. "Totally against the rules. A prosecutor can't just walk out and start flapping his gums about an ongoing criminal case in the press."

"He's trying to get himself elected right now," Jack said. "And it might work. Did you see this story in the paper?"

He slid a copy of the Kingsport newspaper across the desk. In it, on the editorial page, one of the editors had taken it upon himself to write a scathing, accusatory letter to the football players who were at the party.

"You know," part of the letter said. "We know you know, and you need to have the courage to come forward and help the police and Mike Armstrong. Stop protecting the rapists among you."

"Wow," I said. "This is starting to remind me of the Salem witch hunts. It feels like a frenzy, a lynch mob mentality. The university better get its act together and respond to this stuff forcefully, and they better do it in a hurry. Has the coach said anything publicly?"

"He's said he believes his players when they say no assault occurred. At the same time, he's taking responsibility for not maintaining enough control over them and letting this happen in the first place."

"I wonder if he'll be the sacrificial lamb," I said. "The university will be looking for one. They'll fire somebody, and it'll probably be him."

"Probably," Jack said. "Why don't you report Armstrong to the board?"

The "board" to which Jack was referring was the Tennessee Board of Professional Responsibility, an organization in Nashville created to police lawyers across the state. I regarded them as a bunch of ineffective bureaucrats, pencil pushers who'd either never practiced law or had tried it and failed.

"Because I'm not a rat," I said, "and I can't stand the BPR. Don't ever go anywhere near them unless you absolutely have to."

"How did it go with the Davidsons?" Jack said.

"Went good. I like him. I don't think he sexually assaulted anyone."

"So we're going to represent him?"

"We are."

"What about your 'I don't represent accused rapists' rule?"

"Rules change sometimes. Where's Charlie?"

"I think she's in her office."

"Sit tight. I'll be right back."

I walked down the hall to find Charlie staring at her computer screen, no doubt poring over case law. She was a junkie when it came to law. She loved it.

"Could I borrow you for a few minutes?" I said.

She looked up and flashed a beautiful smile.

"Sure. Your office?"

"Conference room."

"Be right there."

I went to the front and asked Beverly and Kelly to come to the conference room.

When everyone was gathered, I sat down at the head of the table. They'd left the seat open for me. I didn't know whether they did it consciously, but they showed me deference and respect on a regular basis. It made me feel good sometimes, but it also embarrassed me to a degree and it made me feel old.

"I'm sure everybody's heard about the ETSU rape case," I said, "and everybody knows I met with Kevin Davidson and his parents. We're going to take it on, but I want all of you to know that this is going to be difficult. Mike Armstrong wants to be elected district attorney. The primary is in the spring and if he wins the primary, he wins the election because there isn't a Democrat in this part of the state that can get elected to any public office. There is nothing worse for criminal defense lawyers than an election. People just aren't themselves when they're running for office. They make bad decisions, stupid choices, and put themselves and their ambition ahead of everything else. What we have brewing at ETSU is potentially a bombshell. I don't want to sound like an alarmist, but with everything that's been going on in this country lately, this is the worst possible time for something like a young black man to be accused of raping a young white woman. The nuts will be coming out of the woodwork. And when I say nuts, I mean extremists of many different kinds. We're going to see feminists going after the administration and the football program and our client, we'll probably see liberal faculty groups going after the team and our client. We're going to see white supremacists going after our client and maybe after his lawyers, so I want you to keep your heads up and watch your backs.

"Somebody at the university will be the scapegoat, and I'm guessing they'll put it on the coaching staff. The head coach will get fired or resign, probably within the week. If this kind of thing runs deep at the university – and I'm talking about accusations of athletes sexually assaulting young women – then a few more heads will roll. But I've never heard any rumblings that the athletes at ETSU are thugs who prey on college girls. This case is more than likely an outlier. After talking with Kevin, I don't think a rape occurred, although just the fact that the football team threw a party with a stripper as entertainment is going to cause a lot of suspicion and a lot of problems for the football team.

"Now, for starters, we need to find out who this woman is that's making the accusations. Kelly, I need you to call Stony and see if she can get on it right away. I want to know everything about her. I also want her to check out Kevin Davidson's background. If there are skeletons in his closet, I want to know about them. Tell her to do her best to find out everything the cops have done.

Jack and Charlie, I want you to go to the neighborhood around Kevin's house and talk to people. Let's find out what they saw and heard the night of the party. I'm sure the cops are already doing the same thing, so they might be reluctant to talk to you, but we have just as much right to conduct investigations as the police, so suck it up and be persistent. Let's try to get ahead of the cops if we can. I also want you to find out which cop was the first to have contact with this girl. Find out if a rape kit was done. Find out if they took blood from her, because if they did, we're entitled to a sample for independent analysis. I'm going to talk to the other two guys that live with Kevin if they haven't hired lawyers. If they have, I'll see if I can talk to them with their lawyers. I'm also going to talk to the football coach and the president of the university to see if they're going to back these guys up or hang them out to dry."

"What about the sheriff's girlfriend?" Jack said.

"Are you talking about Erlene Barlowe?"

"Yeah, she runs a strip club, right? Maybe she knows the stripper."

"She doesn't run an escort service that I know of, but I haven't seen her in a while. Maybe she's expanded her business empire. I'll pay Erlene a visit."

"Where? At her club?"

"Is that a problem?"

"Mom might have a problem with you going to a strip club."

"I've been there before, and your mom knows Erlene. They're friends. Besides, I won't go when they're open. I'll catch her in the afternoon when she's doing her paperwork. That way I won't see any of the girls in action. Will that satisfy you, you prude?"

"Just looking out for Mom," Jack said.

"Your mom trusts me, obviously more than you do. How about this? You can go instead. Charlie, you wouldn't mind if Jack went to a strip club to talk to the owner, would you?"

"Not as long as he wears a blindfold," Charlie said.

I smiled and looked around the table.

"I'll talk to Erlene. The rest of you know what to do. I think we have the rarest of opportunities in the world of criminal defense. We have a client who's actually innocent. There's a downside to our client being innocent, though. It raises the stakes. None of us wants to see a young man go to prison for something he didn't do, and none of us wants to see his future ruined. So, we pretty much have to prove he was innocent, and we have to make the state say it out loud. So let's get our act together and do this right."

THURSDAY, AUGUST 29

I pulled my pick-up truck onto the gravel driveway that wound about two hundred yards through a stand of birch trees, across a narrow creek, and finally crested a ridge before the cabin came into view. It was a little after five o'clock, and the breeze coming out of the west was still warm and smelled of pine. I'd called my sister, Sarah, earlier in the day and asked if I could come down and talk with her. She'd agreed. She didn't ask the purpose of the visit, although I could tell by the tone of her voice over the phone she was curious. She'd moved to this isolated, seven-acre piece of property in southwestern Washington County a couple of years before, and I didn't often get a chance to visit.

As I got closer to the cabin, I noticed movement to my right. A young girl riding a black pony was racing toward me at full gallop. The girl was my seven-year-old niece, Grace, and as I parked the truck and got out, she jumped out of the saddle and into my arms.

"Uncle Joe!" she said, a huge grin crossing her face. "Momma said you were coming to visit!"

"You're growing like a weed, Gracie," I said. The child was nearly a mirror image of her mother, dark haired and dark eyed and dark skinned. She was truly delightful. "What's your pony's name, and when did you learn to ride like that?"

"Her name is Pepper, and I rode every day this summer. She even jumps. Do you want to see her jump, Uncle Joe?"

"Sure, if it's okay with your mother."

"Momma doesn't care if I jump. She thinks it's cool."

Grace led Pepper to a tree stump and climbed back into the saddle. She nudged the pony with her heels and it took off full speed. They headed straight for a line of low, plastic tubes that looked like PVC pipe. The tubes had been fitted into plastic cubes and were about a foot off the ground. Grace and Pepper jumped four of them and were back by my truck two minutes after they took off.

"That was impressive, Grace," I said. "You're quite the little equestrian."

"Eques... what? What's that mean?"

"Equestrian. It means horse rider. You're good at it."

She smiled and nodded her head.

"Where's your mother?" I said.

"She's in the house."

"I'm going to go in and talk to her for a few minutes. Have fun. I'll see you in a little bit. I want to watch you ride some more before I leave."

There was a pick-up truck I didn't recognize, a red one, parked out near the barn and as I walked up toward the cabin. I saw a man I didn't recognize look out at me from just inside the barn. I raised my hand and waved, but he turned around and walked away from me.

I knocked on Sarah's side door and it opened within a couple of seconds.

"Hey, stranger," she said as she reached out to hug me. She gave me a peck on the cheek. "Nice to see you."

"You, too," I said. "You look good."

Sarah was also dark-skinned, dark-eyed and dark-haired. She was tall and lean, and her skin smooth as ever. I always marveled at how Sarah could have spent so many years abusing herself with drugs and alcohol and didn't seem any worse for the wear. I chalked it up to genetics. She was just a beautiful woman, and, it seemed, no amount of self-abuse could overcome the genetic predisposition. She'd spent more than a year in the county jail on a variety of charges when she was younger. She'd caught drug charges, DUIs, theft charges. I knew her self-destructive nature was a result of my uncle raping her when she was a child, and she'd finally seemed to overcome it. She'd been running her diner in Jonesborough for three years. It did well and she worked hard. She and Grace seemed to be doing great, and she'd told me several times how much she loved living in the boonies.

"What can I get you?" Sarah said. "Coffee? Tea? Water? There are a few beers in the refrigerator if you want a beer. And in case you're wondering, no, they're not mine. They're Greg's."

"Who's Greg?"

"A friend. He helps out around the place."

"That's his truck?" I said.

"Yeah."

"I waved at him. He didn't wave back."

"He's shy," Sarah said. "Don't think anything of it."

"Is Greg a boyfriend?" I said.

Sarah smiled. "You never change. Greg's a friend who happens to be a man. He's great with horses and Grace thinks the world of him."

"Good. Does Greg have a last name?"

"Murray. Why do you want to know his last name?"

I shook my head. "Just curious."

"You're going to check him out, aren't you?"

"Not unless you want me to."

"I don't. He's a good guy."

"Okay. Whatever you say. And I'll drink one of his beers if you don't think he'll mind too much."

"He won't."

She popped the top off a long neck Budweiser and handed it to me. Then she poured herself some hot water and dropped a tea bag into the cup.

"He has good taste in beer as far as I'm concerned," I said. "None of this fancy craft stuff for me."

"You're stuck in the past," she said. "Sit, please."

We sat down at her kitchen table. It was a nice little place, her cabin. I'd been there a few times before and loved the rustic feel. And Sarah kept it spotless.

"So what's on your mind, Joe?" she said. "To what do I owe the pleasure of your company?"

"To what do you owe the pleasure of my company? Have you been to finishing school since the last time we talked?" I said.

"No, I'm still a redneck. Nowhere near finished. I just get a kick out of talking that way sometimes. It surprises the hell out of some of my regulars."

"I'll bet. I came down here to tell you I'm going to take on a case, and I want to make sure you're good with it. If you're not, I'll tell the client I changed my mind and I'll move on to something else."

"The rape at ETSU?" she said. "I knew you would wind up involved in that."

"Alleged rape. You know I've never represented anyone accused of rape, and you know why."

"I'm aware you've never represented a rapist, but you didn't have to do it for me."

"I did it for me as much as for you."

"I'm glad you recognize that," she said.

"So you're okay with it?"

"Is he guilty?"

"I don't think so. I really don't."

"Then do that thing you do. Defend the hell out of him. Piscybody else you can along the way."

"I like to think I've toned it down a little over the past few years. You know, mellowing with age."

"You'll never mellow, Joe. You can't stomach injustice. It makes you physically ill. I've seen it plenty of times. You might play a little smarter, you might be a little less rough around the edges, but you'll never mellow. When was the last time you were in a fistfight?"

"It's been a while. But I've been doing some grappling with Jack just to stay in shape."

"Grappling? You mean wrestling?"

"Judo, jujitsu, wrestling, that kind of stuff."

"Jack's big as a house and strong as a bull," Sarah said. "He could turn you into a pretzel."

"I'm not exactly a pushover. I'm older, but I'm nowhere near dead."

"You're crazy is what you are. Rolling around with that brute. Don't let him break your neck."

"I won't. And thank you. I appreciate it, Sarah, I really do. Knowing you're okay with this case will help me do a better job."

"Well, from what I've seen it looks like it's going to be more of a race case than a rape case anyway."

"You may be right."

I finished the beer and stood.

"Gracie has grown so much. And I had no idea she could ride like that."

"You should come by more. She misses you."

"What about you? You miss me?"

"I do, Joe. I miss you and I miss your family. How's Caroline?"

"She's Caroline. The toughest human being I've ever met."

"Give her my love."

"I will."

I stepped out of the house into the lengthening shadows as the sun slowly dropped toward the ridges to the west. Grace rode up again.

"Are you leaving, Uncle Joe?"

"Sorry, sweetie, I have to go. How about showing me those jumps one more time?"

She turned and galloped off. She cleared all of the jumps easily and was back in just a couple of minutes.

"That's really cool, Grace," I said. "I wish I could spend some more time with you."

"Can I come up and swim in your pool soon?"

"Absolutely. You can come swim any time you like. But Labor Day for sure."

I reached out and hugged her and kissed her on the cheek while she was still on the pony.

"You and Pepper have a good evening," I said. "I'll see you again soon. I love you, pretty girl."

"Bye, Uncle Joe," she said as she trotted away toward the barn. "Love you, too."

I looked up at Sarah, who was standing in the doorway. I waved and she waved back. I saw the man, Greg Murray, again, lurking in the doorway to the barn. Something about the guy gave me the heebies.

I raised my hand to him, but he turned his back on me again and disappeared into the barn. I took note of the tag number on his truck and left. As soon as I pulled onto the road, I dialed Leon Bates's cell number.

"Brother Joe Dillard," Leon said in his Southern drawl. "How's it going?"

"Good, Leon, how have you been?"

"Finer than frog hair, brother."

"Good, good to hear. I hate to call you out of the blue and ask for a favor, but I need one."

"Fire away," Leon said.

I gave him the tag number on Greg Murray's truck and told him his name.

"He's hanging around my sister," I said, "and you know as well as I do she doesn't have a sterling record when it comes to men. Would you mind checking to see if this guy has a criminal record?"

"Not at all. Want me to do it right now?"

"Do you have time?"

"Sure. I'll call you back in ten minutes."

"Thank you, Leon."

I disconnected the call. Ten minutes later, he called me back.

"He has a record," Leon said.

"How bad is it?"

"He's only been convicted of one crime. He robbed a bank over in Elizabethton eleven years ago. Didn't use a gun or any other kind of weapon, just handed the teller a note. Walked out the door with a grand total of three thousand dollars. The Elizabethton police arrested him less than a mile away from the bank, so he obviously isn't the brightest crayon in the box. Feds sentenced him to ten years, he served eight years and eight months, then did six more months in a halfway house in Knoxville. He got out of there in June, so he hasn't been around long."

"That's great. A bank robber hanging around my niece and my sister. I wonder if he's a druggie."

"Maybe," Leon said. "Or maybe he just needed a little cash in a hurry and his momma wouldn't loan it to him. You should ask him."

"Oh, don't worry about that, Leon. I'll ask him."

"I'm sure you will. Try not to hurt him too bad when you do."

"Thanks, Leon. You're my man."

"Careful, brother Dillard. People will say we're in love."

FRIDAY, AUGUST 30

I woke up the next morning to the news that every single ETSU football player was voluntarily giving a DNA sample to the police and that the president of the university, an extremely bright and decent man from everything I knew of him, was considering forfeiting the first two games of the football season. I didn't think either was a good idea. Voluntarily giving the samples was voluntarily giving evidence to the police, evidence that, in the wrong hands, could be misinterpreted or, at worst, manipulated or falsified. Forfeiting the first two games sent the message that the administration believed the players were either guilty or otherwise at fault. The paper reported that the forfeits would be "punishment for having a party where the entertainment was provided by an exotic dancer," but there were other ways of doling out punishment for the actions of stupid young men. Forfeiting games affected all of the players, all of the fans, the opposing teams and their fans, the marching bands, the cheerleaders, the people who sold shirts and concessions. It affected thousands of people outside of the players, and I just didn't think it was a good idea. It also ensured that the news coverage, which was building steam every day, would ramp up another notch.

I'd tried to call the president of the university and the football coach the previous afternoon, but I hadn't been able to get them on the phone and neither had returned the call. I guess I had some answers, though. They were throwing their guys under the bus as far as I was concerned. Having them voluntarily submit DNA samples to the police was a public relations move, not something done with the players' best interests in mind. Forfeiting the games – if they did it – was more of the same. They were condemning the players' actions in the public domain. I sat at the kitchen table and thought about the university's dilemma for a few minutes. It was a nightmare. Because of the stupidity of a few young men, an entire institution that employed thousands of people and was one of the most important economic and cultural entities in the area, was going to be put through hell. There were already angry protests being held on campus, calls to disband the football team, an advertisement in the newspaper taken out by thirty members of the faculty that basically called the players rapists and blamed it on the university administration. As I'd mentioned in the meeting at the office, a lynch mob mentality had developed, just as I knew it would. Everyone wanted blood, somebody's blood, and they wanted it now. To hell with the truth; they'd sort that out later.

Caroline came padding in around 6:00 a.m. to get some orange juice so she could take her morning pain medication.

"This thing at ETSU is getting crazier by the second," I said.

"I think somebody's stealing my meds," she said.

I looked up from the paper.

"Are you serious?" I said.

"Remember when I came up short on the 80 milligram pills a few weeks ago and we thought maybe the maid had stolen them at the hotel in Nashville? I don't think it was a maid."

Caroline took a lot of Oxycontin. She had to. There were tumors virtually all over her skeletal system, and if she didn't receive high doses of pain medication, she wouldn't have been able to survive. She took the Oxy in two dosages – one eighty milligram pill in the morning and another at night, and thirty milligram pills for what they called "breakthrough" pain. If she had a lot of pain in her knees or her back or her hips during the afternoon or at night, she could take a thirty-milligram pill and it would usually help. She didn't take the thirties all that often. She'd told me she'd been hoarding them because the doctor prescribed them once a month, the insurance company paid for them, and she picked them up at the pharmacy. What she didn't use, she stashed in a bottle that she kept on her vanity in the bathroom. She never knew when she might need them.

But when the eighties came up missing, she was miserable for more than a week. The kind of pain that cancer causes in a person's bones is the kind of pain you have to stay ahead of. Without the eighties, she got behind, and she suffered tremendously. Twelve pills were gone, and she couldn't just go to the doctor and get another prescription. The insurance company wouldn't let her have more than the prescribed dose, thief or no thief. Oxycontin was heavily regulated, sometimes, I thought, to the point of ridiculousness, but it was being abused all over the country and the government – and the insurance companies – had really cracked down. You couldn't just go to your doctor or to the pharmacy and say, "Somebody stole my eighty-milligram Oxycontin tablets." The doctor couldn't prescribe more, and even if she had, the insurance company wouldn't have paid and the pharmacy wouldn't have dispensed the pills.

"You know how I store up the thirties?" Caroline said. "I should have about ninety of them. I looked last night and I only have around twenty. Somebody's stealing pain medication from a cancer patient, and I think I know who it is."

"Tracey?" I said.

"It has to be."

Tracey Rowland was Caroline's home health care nurse. He'd started coming to the house to give her intravenous sodium chloride after a urinary tract infection dehydrated her so badly she didn't know her name and wound up in the hospital for a week. He was friendly enough, but there were a couple of things that had bothered me about him from the beginning. The first was that he was a pretty boy who gave off a sleazy kind of vibe. He was always chatting and sharing details of his personal life that he shouldn't have been sharing. He was supposed to show up at eight in the morning on Monday and Wednesday, hook up the IV, and leave. The IV usually took about three hours, and I always went home and turned off the machine, unhooked Caroline from the machine, flushed her PICC line, capped it, and we'd have lunch together. But Tracey texted Caroline a lot and even managed to get her to invite him and his wife out to dinner. He acted like he wanted to become a friend of the family, but I just wanted him to do his job. I wasn't jealous of him; he simply made me uncomfortable. I'd mentioned it to Caroline and she agreed that he was a little too friendly, but Caroline wasn't as cynical as I.

The other thing that bothered me about the guy was that he went into our master bathroom, which was where the drugs were, every time he came to the house. He said he was washing his hands, but I noticed he had hand cleaner with him and he always put on gloves. So why all the hand washing? And why in our bathroom? He could have washed his hands in the kitchen or in the half-bath right outside of our bedroom. But he always washed them in our bathroom, and he did it twice during every visit. He washed them as soon as he got there and he washed them right before he left.

"That miserable son of a bitch," I said. "I knew there was something wrong with the guy. I'll break every bone in his body."

"Joe, you can't do that."

"The hell I can't. You were crying when you ran out of the eighties. You were in so much pain you barely slept for a week. If he's doing this, I'm definitely going to see to it that he suffers as much as you did."

"You'll go to jail. And besides, we have to prove it," she said.

"I won't go to jail. First things first. We have to catch him red-handed."

"How do we do that?"

"I guess a nanny cam would probably be best. I'll get Jack to help me set it up. We put it at a good angle and when he goes in to wash his hands, if he's stealing, it'll be on the camera. They're compatible with phones now. I can't wait to sit down with him and show him a video of him stealing your medication. The look on his face will be priceless."

"And then you're going to call the police."

"Not before I hurt him. I can't believe this, baby. A freakin' junkie working as a home health nurse and stealing Oxycontin from a cancer patient. I wonder how prevalent it is."

"I'll bet it happens a lot," Caroline said.

"I'll get a camera today," I said. "We'll catch him."

FRIDAY, AUGUST 30

The Mouse's Tail hadn't changed at all over the past several years. Erlene Barlowe, the owner, put a fresh coat of paint on it every once in a while, but it was still the tacky, unseemly, block building it had always been. There was an awning on the front and an air-brushed painting of a large mouse with a long tail that formed into the shape of an erect penis. I suppose the mouse could have been declared obscene and Erlene could have been forced to remove it, but nobody seemed to care enough to force the issue. The place had been there for a long time, it was in the county, out of sight from the road, and after the initial resistance from the preachers finally died down, people pretty much left Erlene alone to bilk money from horny, lonely, stupid pervs.

I arrived at 1:00 p.m. and spotted Erlene's red Corvette immediately. I hadn't seen her in several months and wanted to surprise her, so I didn't bother to call and tell her I was coming. I walked up to the side door of the building, which is where I knew she entered. It was locked, so I knocked. It opened a minute or so later to reveal a redhead in her early to mid-fifties who looked ten years younger. She was wearing pink spandex pants and a pink, cheetah print blouse that was open at the neck and revealed a large portion of her extremely large breasts. They were natural, by the way. She'd told me so on more than one occasion, and she was extremely proud of them.

"Well, I swan, if it isn't my favorite lawyer in the whole wide world," she said as she opened her arms and squeezed my neck. She gave me a peck on the cheek and stepped back.

"Hi, Erlene," I said. "You're looking outrageously hot, as usual."

"Thank you, sugar," she said. "You look plenty sexy yourself. How's that wonderful wife of yours?"

"She's good, thanks for asking. Still fighting the fight. How are you and Leon getting along?"

"We decided to take a little break, which I think will probably turn into a permanent break," she said.

I was genuinely surprised. She and Leon Bates, the sheriff, seemed well-suited for each other. Any time I'd been around them, they'd acted like teenagers.

"What happened?" I said. "I thought you guys were great for each other."

"I still care a great deal for Leon," she said. "He's a sweetie pie. But the lust started to wear off and then I think we both realized what could happen to his career if people started finding out he was dating me. We just thought it was best to be friends. I take it you haven't seen him lately."

"I talked to him not long ago, but we didn't talk about you. Plus I've been so busy with Caroline and everything that's going on with her. I'll have to call him back and see how he's doing."

"Give him my best when you do," she said. "Come on in here and have a seat. Can I get you something to drink?"

"I'll take a bottle of water if you have one," I said as we walked into the club and I sat down at a table near the bar.

"We don't sell bottled water, sugar. Be happy to get you a glass of ice water, though."

"Sure, thanks."

Erlene brought the water and sat down across from me. As always, I had to force myself to keep from looking at her breasts.

"So what brings you out here?" Erlene said. "Not that you need a reason."

"Have you heard about what's going on at ETSU?" I said.

"Of course," she said. "I don't live in a cave."

"I'm sorry. I wasn't trying to insult you. I just didn't know how much attention you paid to the news. I've been hired to represent a young man who might be charged with raping the dancer that was hired by the football team. He swears he didn't do it, and I tend to believe him. The players pooled their money and hired her through an escort service called AAA Escort. I was wondering if you know anything about the escort service or if you might have heard anything about who the girl is. I don't even know her name yet."

A look of confusion came over her face. It was a look I had never seen. Erlene was an intelligent, even cunning, confident woman. She was not easily confused.

"I seem to remember you telling me that you won't represent men accused of rape," she said.

"I'm making an exception."

"Do you mind if I ask you why?"

"The reason I wouldn't take rape cases is a long story I'd rather not get into, but with Jack and Charlie joining the law firm, Caroline thought I shouldn't limit them because of something that happened in my past. I agreed to talk to this kid and his parents and I liked what I heard. He seems to be a good kid. I don't think he raped anybody."

"Fair enough," she said. "Do you think somebody else raped her?"

"He says no, but I have no idea. That isn't my concern. My concern is to make sure he doesn't get a rape pinned on him if he's innocent."

She nodded her head slowly.

"I have a little surprise for you," she said.

"What's that?"

"You came to the right place, sweetie pie. I own AAA Escort Service."

I was stunned. She had never mentioned owning an escort service. It made sense, but she'd never said a word.

"No kidding? Been in that business a long time?"

"A couple of years. It goes well with what we do here. Extra income for me. Extra income for the girls. They usually make good money."

"So you know who the girl was at the party?"

"I do. I sent her."

"Mind telling me her name?"

"Sheila Elizabeth Self. You'll find out soon enough anyway."

"Has she told you about what happened?"

"She said she was drugged and pulled into a bathroom. She thinks three men raped her, but she's fuzzy about the details."

"What do you think?"

"I don't think she has any reason to lie, sugar. Sheila's had an incredibly difficult life. She's been used and abused by so many people it's a wonder she hasn't killed herself by now. You know how I am about girls like that. I do what I can to help and protect them. And she's trying to keep it together. She graduated from junior college and is working on a degree at ETSU. She has two small children and nobody to help her raise them. I sent her hoping she'd make some decent money. She needs it for those kids."

"Have you heard from the police?"

"Of course. Some skin-headed bully named Investigator Riddle came out here and made a bunch of empty threats. I would have called you if I thought it was anything serious."

"Can I talk to the girl? To Sheila?"

"That'd be up to her, sweetie."

"Put in a good word for me?"

"I'll talk to her, but she's still pretty torn up."

"I appreciate it, Erlene," I said as I rose to leave. "It's good to see you."

"Give Miss Caroline my best," she said.

She walked me to the door, opened it, and as I stepped out into the sunshine, she said, "I hope your client is okay if he didn't do anything to her, but if he did, I hope he burns in hell. And those folks at ETSU? They need to get their ducks in a row. They need to get some control over what's going on over there."

"And what might that be?" I said. "What's going on over there?"

"A lot more than you know."

As I walked across the parking lot to my truck, I could feel Erlene's eyes on me. She had played the Southern belle, honey and sweetie role during our conversation, but she had, for the first time since I'd known her, lost her composure just a bit. It manifested itself as slight confusion, but she'd also gone slightly cold toward me. I could sense it, and that had *never* happened. Erlene knew more than she was telling me. I had a strong sense that I'd be hearing from her in the very near future.

FRIDAY, AUGUST 30

Sheila Self walked into Investigator Bo Riddle's office just after three o'clock in the afternoon and sat down across from Riddle, who was at his desk. Riddle had stayed in regular contact with Sheila since their first interview. He'd kept her up on the progress of the investigation and seemed genuinely interested in helping her find the man or men who had raped her. He also seemed genuinely interested in what was going on in her life and had assured her that he would help her in any way he could. He asked about her children. He asked about her aunt. He asked whether she planned to stay enrolled in school at ETSU. She said she was going to take at least a semester off and see what happened.

"I have some photographs I want to show you," Riddle said after Sheila settled in.

"Okay."

"If you can identify any of the people in the photos as being an assailant, it would go a long way toward helping us make an arrest."

"But I—"

Riddle held up his hand.

"Let me ask you a question," he said. "It might be out of line, but it might not. The answer will also go a long way toward helping me know whether I'm going to become totally committed to this case for you."

"What's the question?"

"How do you feel about black people, in particular, how do you feel about black men?"

Sheila bit her lip and covered her eyes with her hand for a moment. When she pulled her hand back, she looked directly at Riddle and said, "When I was in high school, right here in Johnson City, there were two black guys that wouldn't leave me alone. They snapped my bra, they pinched my ass, they felt my breasts and tried to get their hands down my pants. They were always talking about how much they wanted to have sex with me. None of the white guys would come anywhere near me because they'd heard about what had happened to me with my father and my foster father and brother. I was used goods. But the black guys didn't care. They just kept coming on to me. I went to the principal's office and complained, but both of them were athletes and they wouldn't do anything to them. So finally I put a knife in my purse and brought it to school with me. It was a big knife, a butcher knife I took from the kitchen at the group home where I was living at the time. During lunch, I went outside and here came one of them, a basketball player named Damien Thompson. He walked right up to me and grabbed both of my breasts. I pulled the knife out of my purse and slashed his arm with it. I cut him pretty bad."

"Did he leave you alone after that?"

"Did he leave me alone? He went straight to the office, they called the police, and I wound up getting convicted of aggravated assault. They sent me off to Nashville to the juvenile detention center there, which was awful. I was there for a year."

"I'm sorry," Riddle said. "I wasn't aware of that. We don't really have access to juvenile records. They're not in any database, so when I looked at your NCIC record, it didn't come up. So I guess the answer to my question is that you don't care much for black men."

"I hate them," Sheila said.

Sheila noticed a slight smile come over Riddle's face.

"Okay, I just want you to look at these photos I'm about to show you. And when you're asked about it later, you're going to say you picked the photos you pick out of a large group I showed you. I might coach you a little, but if I do, it's because I'm convinced this is at least one of the people who assaulted you. Can you do that for me?"

"I guess I can, but I still really don't remember very clearly."

"I think this will help. Scoot up close to the desk."

Sheila did as Riddle asked, and he laid out six photographs of young black men in front of her. All of them were in ETSU football uniforms.

"All of these guys were at the party as far as we know," Riddle said. "Take a close look."

Sheila noticed that Riddle had the index finger of his right hand on one particular photograph. He kept tapping it.

"That might be him," Sheila said.

"Which one?"

"The one you're pointing at."

"I'm not pointing at anything," Riddle said as he tapped the photo a little harder. "Now, which one do you think is the one who attacked you?"

Riddle removed his finger from the photo.

"That one," she said, pointing out a photograph of Kevin Davidson.

"How sure are you?"

"Pretty sure."

"Fifty percent? Eighty percent? A hundred percent? It would be perfect if you could say you're a hundred percent sure it was him."

Sheila paused for a minute, playing along. She knew exactly what was going on. She also knew this needed to happen. She scanned the photos one last time, acting as though she were studying the other faces.

"That's him," she said. "He's the guy that pulled me into the bathroom."

"How sure are you?" Riddle said.

"A hundred percent."

"And after he pulled you into the bathroom, this is one of the young men that raped you?"

"Yes. It was him."

"You would swear an oath to tell the truth in court and testify that it was him?"

"I would."

Riddle handed Sheila a felt tipped pen.

"Put an X on the photo, initial it and date it," he said.

Sheila did as he asked.

"Okay, so that's done," Riddle said. "At least we have one of them. But you told Officer James and the people at the hospital that you thought you were raped by three people, so you need to pick two more."

"Which ones?" Sheila said. "I don't really recognize anyone."

Riddle tapped his fingers on the photos of two more of the black players.

"These will do," he said. "But I need to hear you say you're a hundred percent sure and be willing to testify to that in court."

Sheila nodded her head. "Okay. I'm a hundred percent sure and I'll testify."

"Make an X on each, initial and date, just like with the other."

Sheila did as he asked.

"Thank you, Ms. Self," Riddle said. "This takes us another step closer to making sure the right thing gets done."

FRIDAY, AUGUST 30

A s soon as Sheila Self left his office, Investigator Riddle picked up his cell phone and dialed the number of District Attorney General Mike Armstrong. Riddle was almost giddy. Sheila Self actually hated black people as much as he did. It was a tremendous stroke of luck for him.

Mike Armstrong had sensed that the chief of police was not particularly interested in pressing the case, but that Riddle was. Therefore, he'd asked Riddle to personally inform him of any developments and to put together a case as quickly as possible. Riddle knew Armstrong was out on a limb, but Riddle was willing to climb out there with him because of his hatred for both the black football players and the institution they represented.

"Sheila Self just left my office," Riddle said when Armstrong answered the phone.

"And?"

"She positively identified three players that raped her."

"I thought she couldn't remember what happened."

"It's coming back to her. I showed her a group of photos and she picked out three guys."

"How many photos did you show her?"

"At least forty. I showed her white guys and black guys and Hispanics." It was a lie, but Riddle didn't care. He was going to make this case come hell or high water.

"Who are they?" Armstrong asked.

"All three of them are black. The quarterback, Kevin Davidson, a linebacker named Demonte Wright, and a defensive back named Evan Belle."

"Oh, man," Armstrong said. "What a powder keg."

"Do you want me to arrest them?"

"Not yet," Armstrong said. "Keep it under your hat for now, and let's pray to God we get some DNA evidence."

FRIDAY, AUGUST 30

University President Dr. Dean Brady was holding yet another meeting late Friday afternoon with the same group with whom he'd been meeting throughout the week. This meeting, however, would be a bit different.

Seated around the table were George Darden, the university's lead lawyer, Raymond Winters, the athletic director, Blakely Burton, the director of university relations and Mike Springer, the head football coach.

"We might as well get right to it," Brady said. He was a clean cut, handsome man with short, salt and pepper hair parted neatly on the left side of his head. His countenance was that of a banker or a politician who took excellent care of himself. He was partial to bow ties, and was wearing a black and white polka-dotted one at the meeting. "I've had many discussions with the Board of Trustees over the past few days and we've made some decisions. They've been extremely difficult decisions, but I feel we've made them with this university's best interests at heart."

Dr. Brady looked across the table at Coach Springer.

"Coach," he said, "we're going to let you go. I'm sorry, but I can't get past the fact you didn't know that fifty or sixty young men for whom you are ultimately responsible could throw a party involving a stripper. Either your senior leadership let you down, or you haven't taught them how to be leaders. Either way, as much as I hate it, this axe falls on you. We've also decided to forfeit the first two games of the season as punishment to the team for their behavior and to let the community know we're taking this seriously. We're also suspending the three senior captains who hosted the party, Kevin Davidson, Dominic Vasso, and Henry Treadway, for the remainder of the season. We haven't yet decided which one of your assistants will become the interim head coach, but that decision will be made in the next couple of hours. The rest of the staff is safe for now."

Springer looked down at the table and then back up at Brady. Bags had formed under his eyes during the week, Brady noticed, certainly from stress and lack of sleep. His eyes were now glistening with tears.

"I'm sorry I let you down, and I understand to a certain degree," Springer, who, at sixty-two, was still a powerfully built man with a full head of gray hair, said. "I figured this would ultimately fall on me. Part of me accepts it, and part of me doesn't. They're college kids, for goodness sake, and whether you or anyone else wants to believe it or talk about it, they're interested in the opposite sex. And I can't be expected to keep tabs on them twenty-four hours every day. Should they have hired a stripper? No. Should they suffer some consequences for that? Of course, because circumstances arose that have caused the university embarrassment. But there was no rape. There was no crime committed.

I'd bet my life on it. I don't agree with the forfeits and I don't agree with the suspensions. They're too harsh. These guys have already been through the wringer, Dr. Brady. And suspending Kevin and Dominic and Henry for the season, which effectively ends their football careers? That's just heartless. You don't know those guys the way I do. They made a mistake, but they're good kids."

"Coach," Brady said. "You're a good man. I thought that when we hired you and I still feel the same. I know you've been under a lot of strain, but so have all of us, and to be honest, I don't care whether you agree with my decisions. You have two years left on your contract. We discussed simply firing you under the lack of institutional control clause in your contract and not paying you, but instead, we'll be exercising our option under the buyout clause, so we're not just leaving you high and dry. I'll expect you to have your things cleared out of your office by midday tomorrow. That's all, Coach Stringer. I wish you the best. You can go now."

"So that's it?" Stringer said, raising his hands.

"That's it. Please don't make me call the campus police."

Stringer rose from his chair and walked out the door without another word. Brady, along with the rest of the group, watched him go.

"Okay, that's done," Brady said. "Blakely, you and George can go, too. Raymond, you stay."

The university relations director and the university lawyer got up and left, leaving only the athletic director in the office.

"What have you found about Title IX violations? Tell me the damned truth," Brady said.

Winters, a veteran of the bureaucratic wars in college athletics, simply shook his head.

"I practically threatened to kill Rhonda James with my bare hands if I found out she was hiding anything," Winters said.

Rhonda James was the Title IX administrator at the university, in charge of documenting and conducting investigations of claims of sexual abuse against female students.

"And she said there's nothing?"

"She has no way of knowing if a tennis coach or a baseball coach or basketball coach hid something," Winters said. "But we don't have anything ongoing, and we don't have anything unresolved or suspicious that I'm aware of."

"Have you talked to the coaches?"

"Every damned one of them. I made sure they knew if we found out they've hidden something, they'd be out on their ass."

"Good," Brady said. "I appreciate it. We've done what we can do. We've taken affirmative action. Now I guess we just hunker down and see if the storm passes."

MONDAY, SEPTEMBER 2

Caroline Dillard watched from the bedroom window while the small, white car with "LifeCare" painted on the side pulled into the driveway. It was Labor Day, but she needed her fluid infusion and the home health care service worked on holidays. Joe had gone into town to run a few errands, but Caroline suspected he was afraid of what he might do or say to Tracey Rowland.

As always, she'd unlocked the front door and shut Rio in the garage. He was going nuts, barking and growling. Caroline had tried to introduce Rio to Tracey. With almost everyone, once they were in the house and Rio had a chance to sniff them and size them up, he tended to leave them alone. He would always bark when someone pulled into the driveway or came to the front door, but he was just doing what German shepherds do – protecting his territory. Once the person got inside the house, he was friendly.

But not with Tracey. There was something about Tracey that made Rio crazy. When Caroline, and even Joe, had tried to introduce Tracey to the dog, the hair on his back bristled and he growled. Caroline knew if Rio got an opportunity, he would sink his teeth into whatever part of Tracey he could. Tracey laughed it off and acted as though it didn't bother him, but Caroline knew he was terrified of the animal, as well he should be. Rio and Joe had a lot in common. They were both fiercely loyal, they were intelligent, and they had an amazing instinct when it came to judging people's character. Rio obviously didn't think much of Tracey, and now Caroline knew why.

Joe and Jack had installed the tiny camera above the vanity in the bathroom where Caroline kept the bottle of thirty milligram Oxycontin pills. They'd done an excellent job of hiding it, because when Caroline went into the bathroom and looked after Joe told her they were finished installing the camera, she couldn't see it even though she knew it was there. Before Joe had left for the office that morning, he and Caroline had gone into the bathroom, emptied the contents of the pill bottle onto the vanity, and counted them in plain view of the camera. Then they returned them to the bottle. The plan was to let Tracey into the house, allow him to do what he always did, and then, after he left, Joe and Jack would hook the camera to Joe's phone and watch the video. If Tracey stole drugs – and Caroline was sure he would – they would pour out the pills and count them again.

Caroline was worried about what would happen. Joe was angry, but Jack, after Joe told him what was going on, had become furious. Jack was as protective of his mother as Joe was of his wife, and Caroline was genuinely concerned that one or both of them would seriously injure Tracey and that they would wind up either paying tens of thousands of dollars in medical bills, perhaps wind up in jail, or, even worse, put their law licenses in jeopardy. She didn't want any of those things to happen, but neither did she want Tracey to continue to steal medication from her. She was also sure that if he was stealing from her, he was stealing from others.

She walked to the front door and opened it just as Tracey walked up onto the porch. He was a decent looking man in his mid-30s, lean and average height. His hair was sandy blond and he wore it long. Sometimes he wore a man bun, which Caroline found extremely unattractive and which Joe found utterly repulsive. His eyes were a pretty, forest green and he sported a closely-trimmed stubble of beard. He was wearing light blue medical scrubs. It was as though he was trying very hard to look macho, but Caroline had been around him enough to know he was far from macho. She was married to macho. This guy was a cupcake compared to Joe.

"Good morning, Caroline," Tracey said as he walked into the house.

"Morning, Tracey."

"And how are we feeling this morning?"

"As well as can be expected under the circumstances."

"When do you have to go back to Nashville?"

"I'm off this week. We go back next Tuesday."

Caroline went into the bedroom and sat down. Joe had bought her a mattress that was adjustable so she could raise her head and her feet, something that had helped make her far more comfortable than lying flat on her back. She climbed into bed and turned on the television.

"Let me just run in and wash my hands and we'll get started," Tracey said.

"Okay."

He disappeared into the master bathroom, like he always did, and was back in about four minutes. He cleaned his hands with hand cleaner, put on a pair of latex gloves, and began to run the plastic tubing through the IV tower that regulated the flow of the sodium chloride that would be running into Caroline's body. Caroline had a PICC line (Peripherally Inserted Central Catheter) that had been inserted into her cephalic vein several years earlier. The PICC line ran to her heart and allowed medical people to give her various medications without having to stick needles into her all the time, something which had once caused her veins to begin to collapse. She didn't like the PICC line because she had to keep it covered with some kind of sleeve all the time, but it was better than being constantly stuck with needles.

Tracey flushed the PICC line and hooked up the tubing that led from the bag of fluid to the PICC line. He turned on the machine, set it to the proper flow, and removed his gloves.

"Is Joe coming home to unhook you or do you want me to come back in three hours?" Tracey said.

"Joe will do it. Thanks."

Tracey removed his gloves, tossed them into a trash can, and returned to the bathroom.

He came back out a couple of minutes later and said, "Well, I guess I'll see you Wednesday then, right?"

"Tracey, is there anything you need to tell me?" Caroline said.

A look of concern came over his face.

"I'm not sure I understand," he said.

"I think I'm missing some medication."

"What kind of medication?"

"Oxy."

"Are you sure?"

"Pretty sure."

"Why are you asking me about it?" he said. His demeanor had very quickly turned to defensive.

"I'm just asking if there's something you need to tell me. Do you have a problem with drugs? Are you addicted? Are you taking my medication?"

"No, I'm not addicted. No, I'm not taking your drugs, and frankly, I'm offended that you'd even ask me a question like that."

"If you're taking my drugs, Tracey, we'll eventually find out," Caroline said. "I haven't said anything to Joe yet, but if you're taking my drugs and he finds out you're taking my drugs, you'll have to deal with him, and I promise it won't go well for you. I've been married to Joe for almost thirty years and I know how he'll react. It'll be violent."

"Maybe you should ask LifeCare for another nurse," Tracey said.

"Do I need to?"

"It seems pretty obvious to me that you don't trust me."

"I don't know what to think. All I know is that some of my pain medication has gone missing, and you're the only person who is around it besides me and Joe."

"Maybe Joe is taking it."

"Joe doesn't take drugs. He wouldn't."

"Well, you might just be surprised. He's been under a lot of pressure. People under a lot of pressure do strange things sometimes."

"Did I just hear you blame me and my cancer for turning my husband into a drug addict and a thief?"

"I'm just saying you never know."

"I do know. It isn't him. And if it isn't you, then someone is sneaking in when we're not around. It has to be someone who knows us well. I'm sorry, Tracey. I didn't mean to accuse you of anything. It's just disturbing to think that someone is stealing from me. I hope you'll forgive me."

"Of course, Caroline. I understand."

"See you Wednesday, then?"

"Nine o'clock, on the dot."

Caroline watched him walk out of the room. Her heart was pounding. How dare he accuse Joe of being a thief and drug addict? She'd tried to give him an out, tried to offer help. But if he was a junkie, she knew he didn't want help. She also knew he'd be back to steal more drugs on Wednesday.

And if the camera showed what she thought it was going to show, Joe, and probably Jack, would be waiting for him.

MONDAY, SEPTEMBER 2

I smoked a pork shoulder in the Big Green Egg on the deck, and the family gathered on Monday afternoon. It was a beautiful day; the sun was shining, and the temperature was in the low eighties. Jack and Charlie, along with Gracie, were swimming in the pool, Caroline was lounging in a chair, and I was keeping myself busy getting all of the food ready. Sarah was in the kitchen helping me. I was a little distracted because I'd watched the video from the nanny cam. It clearly showed Tracey Rowland stealing drugs.

"What's wrong with you?" Sarah said as she began peeling hard-boiled eggs that would soon become deviled eggs.

"We have a little problem with a thief," I said.

"A thief?"

"Yeah, the worst kind of thief. A nurse who steals pain medication from his cancer patient."

"Who? The home health care nurse?"

"Yeah."

"Are you sure?"

"I have it on video. Her meds have been coming up missing, so Jack and I put a nanny cam in the bathroom. We figured it had to be him. He came this morning, and sure enough, he went into the bathroom and stole Oxycontin."

"Have you called the police?" Sarah said.

"Not yet. I want to talk to him first. He'll be back Wednesday morning."

"And you'll be waiting for him, won't you?"

"Sure will."

"You probably don't want to hear this, but you should try to go easy on him," she said. "I was an addict once. I know how it is. Maybe you can get him some help."

I looked over at her and shook my head.

"He hurt Caroline," I said. "You weren't here when she was crying from the pain because she didn't have her medication."

"I didn't know anything about that," she said. "You didn't tell me."

"We haven't exactly been staying in close contact. You work hard, you live in the boonies. I work hard, I take care of Caroline the best I can, I live in the boonies. We've kind of drifted apart over the last couple of years."

"Yeah, life happens," she said.

"I thought you might bring Greg," I said.

She paused for a few seconds.

"I asked him, but he said he didn't think you'd want him around."

"Really? Why would he say that?"

"Because he's a convicted felon. He said it might cause a problem with you."

"Why would he think that?"

"You have a bit of a reputation, Joe. Some people think you run a little hot."

"What did he do?"

"Robbed a bank over in Elizabethton almost ten years ago. He spent more than eight years in the federal pen in Beckley. He did five years in the medium security behind the walls and then they moved him out to the minimum security camp."

"Why'd he rob the bank?"

"The same reason I stole from Mom and from you back in the day. The same reason Caroline's nurse is stealing from her. He was an addict."

"He's clean now?"

"Yeah."

"And you're comfortable with him being around Gracie?"

She stopped peeling the eggs and turned around to face me.

"Isn't the answer to that question obvious, Joe? Of course I'm comfortable with him being around Gracie. If I wasn't, he wouldn't be anywhere near her. He's been great to Gracie. He's been great to me."

"How'd you meet him?" I said.

"He came into the diner and asked me if I had a job open. Said he'd do anything: wash dishes, sweep and mop, cook, clean the toilets. He was open about having just gotten out of prison. I liked him, so I gave him a job."

"And things are heating up between the two of you?"

"We're friends, Joe. We're becoming closer friends, but I'm not sleeping with him or anything. He's been a huge help around the house and with Gracie's horse. He says he grew up with horses. He knows a lot about them."

"Where'd he grow up?"

"Over in Carter County. Buck Mountain."

"Pretty rough place, from what I've always heard."

"That's what he says, but he's really nice. He's quiet and polite and intelligent. He reads a lot. Not what you'd expect from somebody from Buck Mountain who's spent nearly a decade in prison."

I walked over and pulled a pan of baked beans out of the oven, set them on the counter, and covered them in aluminum foil.

"I'll help you with those eggs," I said.

"Are you satisfied with what I told you about Greg?" Sarah said.

"All I want is for you and Grace to be happy and safe," I said.

"Did you already know about him before I told you?"

"Some."

"How'd you find out?"

"I had a friend run his tag after I came down there last week."

"And you've been waiting to have this conversation ever since?"

"Yeah, I guess so. I'm not trying to interfere—"

"Yes, you are."

"No, really—"

"It's okay, Joe. I know you're just concerned. But everything is fine."

"If you say so."

"I say so. He's a good guy who made a terrible mistake. It happens."

WEDNESDAY, SEPTEMBER 4

W hen Tracey Rowland showed up on Wednesday morning, I was waiting for him. The video very clearly showed that both times Tracey went into the bathroom, he turned on the water, grabbed the bottle of Oxycontin, poured a few into his hand, put them in his pocket, put the bottle back, and turned off the water. He didn't even bother to wash his damned hands.

Caroline and I had battled heatedly over what I was going to do. I wanted to tear his head off, and I knew I was perfectly capable of doing so. She wanted me to call the police and have him arrested on Tuesday. We wound up compromising. I promised I wouldn't assault him, but I wanted to at least confront him face-to-face. I'd also had to beg Jack to stay away. He desperately wanted to hurt this man who had caused his mother so much pain and anguish.

Caroline chose to stay in the bedroom with the door closed. Rio was raising hell in the garage. Tracey looked surprised when I opened the front door.

"Hey Joe," he said. "Decide to sleep in this morning?"

"Nah, I was up around five, just like every other day. I have something I want to show you."

"Yeah? What's that?" I detected a bit of trepidation in his voice. He knew something was up.

"C'mon into the kitchen. It's a short video on my phone. I'll show it to you and we can talk."

"What kind of video?"

I walked toward the kitchen and he followed me. I sat down and picked my phone up off the table. I pulled up the video of him stealing the drugs and showed it to him. To my surprise, he showed no reaction.

"I don't understand what you're showing me," he said.

"Are you out of your damned mind?" I said. "That's you stealing my wife's pain medication. You know exactly what it is. Are you selling it or are you addicted?"

"No. That isn't me. It just looks to me like some guy washing his hands. You can't even tell it's me."

"I promised Caroline I'd try to remain civil, but I swear to God if you deny it again I'm going to slap you in the mouth."

He stood immediately.

"You can't threaten me like that," he said.

"I can do more than threaten you. I look at this as defense of another. I think I'd be well within my rights to beat you within an inch of your life and there isn't a jury in the world that would convict me. Hell, with the connections I've made over the years around here, I wouldn't even get charged, not after the DA sees this video and I tell my good friend the sheriff what's been going on around here. Do you have any idea how much pain you caused Caroline when you stole her eighties?"

"I didn't steal anything," he said. "And you can take your threats and your ugly-assed wife and go straight to hell. I'll never set foot in this house again."

That did it. I snapped.

"You're right about that," I said.

I was out of my chair and within striking range in less than a second. I punched him squarely in the nose so hard that blood immediately spurted into the air and he wound up on his back on the kitchen floor.

"Get up, you miserable bastard," I said, reaching down to pull him off the floor. "Get up and get out of here before I kill you with my bare hands."

I pulled him up and dragged him toward the front door. He was bleeding like a stuck hog on the tile and hardwood floor and mumbling that he was going to sue me and have me arrested. When I got to the door, I opened it with my left hand. Then I took a handful of his shirt at the back of his neck in my left hand and grabbed his pants at his lower back with my other hand. I picked him up off the ground and slung him off the front porch. He landed in the grass with a thud.

"You'll be arrested by late this afternoon," I said. "Your job will be gone before you get out of the driveway. And you can kiss your nursing license goodbye. Now get off of my property before I decide I need to beat on you some more."

He managed to climb to his feet and staggered off toward his car with his hands over his nose.

I turned around to see Caroline standing just inside the door.

"You promised," she said.

"Did you hear what he said?"

"Yes."

"Then you understand. There's no way he talks about you that way and walks out without bleeding."

"He's a junkie, Joe. He's in denial. He needs help."

"Junkies don't want help. They're beyond help. Besides, he just got some help. Maybe that'll wake him up a little."

"Are you still going to have him arrested?"

"You're damned right I am. If I don't, he'll just go steal from somebody else."

Caroline sighed and said, "I guess you're right." She turned and walked back toward the bedroom and I went to the kitchen and picked up my cell phone. I dialed Leon Bates's number.

"Brother Joe Dillard," Leon said when he answered. "What's going on today?"

"Hey Leon," I said. "How are you?"

"Better than I deserve, brother. Better than I deserve."

"I'm sorry to bother you with this, Leon, but I have a little problem."

"Always at your service, you know that."

"I need someone arrested as soon as you can get to it. He's Caroline's home health care nurse. Guy named Tracey Rowland. He's been stealing her pain medication. I have him on video doing it. We just caught him. As a matter of fact, he just left our house."

"What kind of shape was he in?" Leon said. He knew me well.

"Not great. He may have a deviated septum. He was bleeding quite a bit."

"He should be more careful," Leon said. "Watch where he's going. What'd he trip over?"

"Something in the kitchen."

"Say he just left there? What company does he work for?"

"It's called 'LifeCare.'"

"Do you have an address and phone number for him?"

"Phone number, no address."

"Not a problem. We'll find him. I'll send one of my investigators over to take a report and get a copy of that video. I'd do it myself but I have to meet with the county budget committee today. Gotta do a little politicking to make sure we get our fair share."

"I appreciate it, Leon. Listen, I talked to Erlene last Friday and she told me you guys split up."

"Yeah, it just wasn't going to work out in the long run. We're still buddies, though. No hard feelings on either side. She knows I'd still do anything for her."

"Good. Glad to hear that."

"What about that mess over at ETSU?" Leon said. "Are you going to get caught up in that?"

"I might. That's what I was talking to Erlene about."

"She help you out?"

"Yeah, but I got the feeling she was holding some things back."

"Well, brother, there's one thing I learned about her for sure. She's sweet as she can be, but there's a dark side to her. You never know what's going through that woman's mind."

"Oh, I'm with you there. I guess I'll just have to wait and see what shakes out."

"Good to talk to you, brother Dillard. I'll get somebody on this drug-stealing nurse right away. Don't be a stranger."

WEDNESDAY, SEPTEMBER 4

W e'd scheduled a meeting for 11:00 a.m. at the office, and I walked in at 10:45 after speaking – along with Caroline – to Leon's investigator. He called me less than five minutes after I talked to Leon and showed up about twenty minutes later. He assured me that he would arrest Tracey Rowland that afternoon, call his employer, and get ahold of the Nursing Board.

As soon as I walked in, Jack came straight into my office. He was practically foaming at the mouth.

"What happened?" he said. "Did he show up?"

"Yeah."

"Did you show him the video?"

"I did."

"What did he say?"

"He said it wasn't him."

"Are you kidding me?"

"No, and then he got mouthy."

"You hit him, didn't you?"

I nodded and held up my right hand, which was still red and swollen. I'd really hit the guy hard.

"Good. Good for you, Dad. Did you break his jaw?"

"His nose."

133

"Did he bleed?"

"A lot."

"Is Mom mad at you?"

"I don't think so."

"Is he going to be arrested?"

"Yes."

"What'll they charge him with?"

"Misdemeanor theft. That's all they can do. He won't do any jail time, but he'll be on probation and have to pass drug tests, they might require him to go to rehab, and they'll take his nursing license. I guess all that, plus a flattened nose, is enough."

"I wish I could have been there," Jack said.

"It was good you weren't there. You have no clue how dangerous you can be when you get angry, and you would have gotten angry."

"I'm not any more dangerous than you are."

"You're bigger, you're stronger and you're younger. You're also impervious to pain. I wouldn't want to fight you."

"Sissy."

"I said I wouldn't *want* to fight you. I didn't say I wouldn't kick your ass. Is everybody ready to go?"

"I think so. Stony's here."

"Great. Let's get to it."

When I walked into the conference room, Kelly Sims, our paralegal was there to take notes. Jack and Charlie were also seated at the table, along with Susan Stoneman, the former FBI agent turned private investigator. I'd previously used a retired Tennessee Highway Patrolwoman named Diane Frye, who had the instincts of a ferret and was, to put it mildly, a bit on the eccentric side, but Diane had become the victim of early-onset Alzheimer's and could no longer work. Stony was a bit more of a tight ass than Diane, but I'd never met an FBI agent who wasn't a tight ass. They were expected to be perfect when they were on the job, so tight ass simply became part of their personality. Stony had lightened up a little since her retirement, but her idea of loose was closer to my idea of grim.

"So," I said when I sat down. "Let's start with Jack and Charlie. I know you talked to Kevin Davidson's neighbors. What'd you find out?"

Charlie and Jack looked at each other, waiting for the other to speak. Finally, Jack nodded and Charlie cleared her throat.

"First thing is the neighbors don't like the football players living there," she said. "So there's some inherent bias. But, on the other hand, they said they're not that bad. They get a little rowdy after games sometimes but always shut it down by midnight, and they throw two big parties a year. Those have gotten out of hand a couple of times and the police were called. As far as what happened Saturday night and early Sunday morning, they just don't know much. From what the neighbors say, and we talked to ten of them, at least from the outside, it appears the players are giving a pretty accurate account of what happened. People started showing up around eight. They were drinking and music was playing. The crowd kept growing. The estimates we got were anywhere between sixty and a hundred people were there at midnight.

"A couple of the neighbors were watching when a cab pulled up at midnight and a girl dressed like a hooker got out. Red spandex dress, spiked heels, fishnet stockings, bling, the whole nine. Everybody piled into the house – the neighbors heard some people talking about a stripper about to perform – and then, about fifteen minutes later, the girl comes back out. She's staggering around and yelling at people who have followed her out of the house. Some of the players are yelling back at her, demanding their money back. One neighbor told me she saw the girl throw a wad of cash at a couple of guys. There were some racial slurs, and they weren't from the players. She was calling several of the players the "n" word. She wound up staggering off up the street, and the next thing the neighbors knew, everybody was gone. They said the place cleared out quickly, like they thought the cops might show up. They said every light in the house went off and there wasn't a car in the driveway or out front in the street."

"And this took how long?" I said. "Did you say fifteen minutes?"

"That's their estimate. About fifteen minutes."

"Did the cops come?"

"Not that we can find. No 911 calls were made."

"So, if we believe what the girl supposedly told the police," I said, "she shows up, goes in and introduces herself, gets paid, disappears for a few minutes, comes back out hammered, is unable to perform, gets dragged into a bathroom and raped by three different players, and is back out the door in fifteen minutes. Talk about premature ejaculation. Those boys were quick."

I looked around the table. Everyone was smiling except for Stony.

"Aw, c'mon, Stony," I said. "That was at least a little funny."

"I don't know that I find it appropriate to joke about gang rape," Stony said.

"The whole point is that there was no gang rape," I said. "Didn't happen. Couldn't have happened. What have you learned about this so-called victim?"

Stony was an open, unapologetic lesbian, which probably also contributed to her serious nature, given the macho environment at the FBI. I was sure she'd taken her share of barbs over the years, and was probably expected to work harder and better than the men with whom she was competing in order to advance. She was forty-seven, about five feet eight inches tall. Her hair was short and wavy, a dark brown, and her eyes were brown. She wore fashionable, dark-rimmed glasses and understated make-up.

"She's a mess," Stony said. "I actually feel sorry for her." She tossed a couple of photos on the table and we started passing them around.

"She looks like a Playboy bunny," Jack said.

"Read a lot of Playboy, do you?" Charlie said.

"No, I don't read Playboy. I just look at the pictures."

The girl was certainly pretty. Red hair, beautiful blue eyes, a face structured like a runway model, full lips, and a body that would make ninety-nine percent of men do a double take.

"Meet Sheila Elizabeth Self. She's twenty-four. Born to an alcoholic mother and a burglar father. The father dropped out of the picture when she was three. Two years later, he was shot dead in a bar in Jackson, Tennessee. When she was twelve, she developed large breasts and her stepfather apparently couldn't keep his hands off of her. He raped her. Her mother wouldn't do anything about it, but she had the courage and the confidence to call the police. The father was ultimately arrested and convicted of aggravated rape. The girl even testified at the trial. He's up for parole in five months. Sheila was removed from the home by Child Protective Services and taken in by a foster family. She must really be unlucky, because a year later she was raped by both her foster father and her foster brother, who was seventeen. They did it on the same night, at the same time, in the same bed, after they got some alcohol and some cocaine into her and into themselves. The foster mother had gone to Indiana to visit her sister. Sheila called the cops again. The foster father is in prison. The brother made a deal and is on parole, a registered sex offender.

"They moved her to another foster home, and she seemed to be getting along all right until she had an incident at school. She began reporting that two black boys were sexually assaulting her. There were multiple reports documented in the school's files. The school administration either didn't want to listen to her because of her past or they wanted to keep these two guys out of trouble. One was a football player and the other a basketball player. She wound up bringing a butcher knife to school and when the basketball player grabbed her breasts one day, she slashed his arm so badly he almost bled to death. They charged her with aggravated assault, adjudicated her to be delinquent, and shipped her off to Nashville until her eighteenth birthday. She came back here, started stripping and prostituting herself, and has had a couple of kids. Along the way, she earned a GED, an associate's degree, and had enrolled at ETSU this semester. I'm guessing she'll drop out. Her declared major is psychology."

As I listened to Stony describe the tortured life of this young woman, my mind wandered a little. I was thinking about how the world could be so random and cruel. She was born with physical beauty, something so many long for, and look what it had cost her. It had cost her a chance of having a normal, happy life. Had she not been born into poverty, had her parents stayed together, had her step father not been a child molesting pervert, her life would have most likely been far different. Maybe at some point in the future she would be able to settle down, like Sarah, and put the demons behind her. But something told me that time would be far in the future for Sheila Elizabeth Self.

"So, she has a motive to lie about being raped by black men," I said. "She probably hates black men."

"My guess is that she hates all men."

I nodded. "Can't say as I blame her."

Stony was able to provide us with a copy of the results of her tox screen from the hospital the night she was arrested.

"How did you get this?" I said.

"That's none of your business. I just thought you might like to have it."

"Absolutely. Thank you. Well, I guess this explains at least part of the behavior. Ecstasy and alcohol? Powerful combination, but we need the blood results from the lab. I managed to get an order from Judge Neese to get a sample from the lab the cops sent it to. Normally, since Kevin hasn't been charged, I wouldn't have been able to get it, but since the lab discards the samples after thirty days, she made an exception. We should be getting the results soon."

"Ms. Self has been talking quite frequently to Investigator Riddle," Stony said. "I think he's coaching her. He showed her a lineup on August twenty-ninth and she picked out three black football players, one of whom is your client. Riddle only showed her six photos, all of them black ETSU football players. I think there might be a secret recording of it."

"How can you *know* that?"

"I have friends inside the department, lots of them, and many of them aren't too happy with the way Riddle is conducting this investigation. They don't like Riddle personally, either. They think he's a racist. Let's leave it at that for now. If I have to tell you more later, I will."

"Was this secret recording audio or video or both?" I said.

"I've been led to believe it contains both."

"Can you get your hands on a copy?"

"I'm working on it."

"What else?" I said, looking at Jack.

"We have some cell phone videos of the party," he said. "Kevin gave us some names, and we hit pay dirt on one of them. The video shows her showing up, disappearing into the bathroom for about eight minutes, the dance that wasn't a dance, the argument, and it shows her stumbling out the door. She didn't even go into the bathroom after the dance."

"You're kidding me," I said.

Jack was smiling.

"It'll go a long way toward discrediting everything she said."

"I talked to Erlene Barlowe, and no, Jack, I didn't see anybody stripping while I was there. I did see more of Erlene's breasts than I cared to, but that's just the way it goes with Erlene. She wasn't much help. She owns AAA Escort Service, though, and she's on Sheila Self's side. Erlene is extremely protective of her girls. She's almost a surrogate mother to a lot of them, although being a semi-pimp doesn't exactly go along with being a mother."

"Does Erlene think she was raped?"

"She says she does, but I don't know how sincere she was about it."

"What the hell is going on here, Dad?"

"I don't know, but I'm going to go see Mike Armstrong and try to stop this before it gets any worse. I don't see how it's possible there will be DNA evidence if she never even went into the bathroom after the dance. Mike needs to shut this down."

"Can Jack and I go with you?" Charlie said.

"Have you ever had a one-on-one with Mike Armstrong?" I said.

"No."

"Neither have I. I've talked to him a couple of times, but he's only been the D.A. for six months, and I haven't had a reason to meet with him one-on-one. Let's just go make a party out of it."

THURSDAY, SEPTEMBER 5

I n a small, white block building that formerly served as a Pentecostal Church off Buck Mountain Road in the mountains of Carter County, Tennessee, Garrett Brown gathered with eight other men at nine o'clock at night. All but three of the men were locals from Carter County. They were members of the Ku Klos Knights of the Ku Klux Klan. One was Brown's closest friend, another his younger brother, and two were his cousins. One of those cousins was an investigator with the Johnson City Police Department named Bo Riddle. The other two outsiders were also brothers. They hailed from Pulaski, Tennessee, a town of about 8,000 citizens located approximately a hundred miles south of Nashville and thirty miles north of the Alabama state line. Pulaski was also the home of the Ku Klux Klan, and the two men who were visiting were leaders in what was now known as The Knight's Party.

Garrett Brown had contacted Josiah and Tobias Gibson after reading the stories in the Johnson City and Elizabethton newspapers regarding the alleged sexual assault of a white woman by at least one, and possibly more, black football players from ETSU. He'd expected to see men dressed like soldiers walk through the door. Instead, these two looked like lawyers in their navy-blue suits and white button-down shirts.

A thunderstorm had rolled across the mountains, and rain was pounding on the roof. An occasional crack of thunder made the small building shudder. Josiah Gibson, who was the older of the two brothers, stood and prayed to open the meeting. He was a small man, almost frail, with pale skin and a thin mustache above his upper lip. When he was finished praying, he said, "Brother Brown, we appreciate your invitation to visit with you and to pray about the situation in which we find ourselves. We also appreciate the attendance of the other brothers you've gathered. Our country is being taken from us, and we have to find a way to stop it. The constant growth of the immigrant population, coupled with the energizing of the Black Lives Matter movement, has slowly been pushing the white agenda to the side in the halls of our politicians. Before long, we'll be pushed all the way out of the building. We must fight back through education and spreading our message to the masses. We must stop the advancement of the liberal agenda. We have to beat them at their own game."

"Forgive me, Brother Gibson," Garrett Brown said, "but I called you because we have a crisis on our hands." Brown was a bear of a man, a logger by trade, who wore a red flannel shirt, blue jeans and boots. His hands were massive and calloused. His hair was long, brown and greasy beneath a John Deere cap, and he'd grown a long, thick, bushy beard. "It's very possible that a young white woman was raped by one, possibly more, niggers who play football for the university in Johnson City. If that happened, and we should know more very soon, then we're not interested in spreading literature or educating anyone. We're interested only in vengeance, the kind that will get the attention of every black son of a bitch in this country."

"You're looking for a war, Brother Brown?" Gibson said.

"You're damned right I am," Brown said, his voice rising. "The climate is right. With all of the militant niggers out there feeling empowered by the liberal agenda that's been stuffed down our throats for the past eight years, I think they'll react violently if we lynch one of these football players and leave him hanging in a public place. The fight will be on, and white America is ready. I've been proud to be an American nearly all of my life. But in the past eight years, with that monkey in the white house, we've been neutered. At least, thank God, he wasn't able to take our guns. We're armed to the teeth and ready for what's coming. I say we light a match to this powder keg we have right here under our noses. They think they sent a message in Ferguson? Wait until they see what kind of message they get from us when this steps off."

"You really think you can start a race war, Brother Brown? Here? Over this incident? My understanding is that the girl is a stripper and may be a prostitute as well."

"So? What difference does that make? She's white, they're black, they raped her, and that's all that matters."

"You're expecting black militant groups to gather here, armed, and start a shootout with white people?"

"We'll hold rallies in support of the lynching. I'll send them emails and post on their websites. That'll bring them out of the woodwork. They're all over the country now: The Nation of Islam, The New Black Panther Party, All Eyes on Egipt Bookstore, Israel United in Christ. They'll come, and they'll be itching to fight. We'll be itching to accommodate them. We have brothers all over Northeast Tennessee, chapters here and in Erwin and in Hampton and in Church Hill, and I have contacts all over the south."

"And you believe the government will let this happen?"

"To hell with the government. They've been part of the problem, not part of the solution."

"If you start a shooting war, Brother Brown, the police will shoot, too. The governor may call in the National Guard. If it gets bad enough, I wouldn't be surprised to see soldiers from the 82nd Airborne Division at Fort Bragg or the 101st Airborne at Fort Campbell come rolling in."

"White American soldiers are not going to fire on white patriots," Brown said. "Besides, it won't come to that. We'll kill so many of them before the soldiers get here that they'll crawl back in their holes and never come out again, and we'll disappear into thin air."

"After you bury your dead. What is it exactly you want from us?" Gibson said.

"A promise that when the shooting starts, you'll bring as many armed men as you can gather and come a running. We'll need to overwhelm them."

Gibson looked at his brother, who hadn't said a word during the entire exchange, and then looked back at Brown. He sighed deeply.

"While I understand your frustration and your anger, and while I sympathize deeply with you, I'm afraid that lynching will only take us backwards. Starting a shooting war will only take us backwards. Violence is not the answer. This fight has to be won in the halls of our lawmakers and in the hearts and minds of our young people."

Brown was stunned. This was nothing like what he had expected.

"So you're just going to turn us down flat?" he said. "You're not going to help?"

"We'll help," Gibson said. "Just not in the way you'd like."

"Well, what do you think about that, fellas?" Brown said. "The men from the birthplace of the mighty Ku Klux Klan are pacifist pussies. You're no better than traitors."

Brown pulled a long-barreled revolver from the small of his back and pointed it at Josiah Gibson's head. The room went silent.

"I'm going to give you and your mute brother ten seconds to get out of here," Brown said. "And if I hear another word out of that pie hole of yours, I'll shut it permanently."

The brothers scrambled to the door and disappeared into the storm.

"That right there exactly what I've been talking about," Brown said to the others after the door had closed. "They're the reason we've gotten to this point, the reason we've lost all of our power. Literature. Education. Hearts and minds. What a bunch of bullshit."

He looked around the room at his men.

"I can count on you when the time comes, right?"

Each man in the room nodded and murmured something affirmative.

"That's good, because if one of you decides you don't have the stomach for what's about to happen, you're gonna meet Mr. Smith and Wesson, and the meeting won't have a happy ending."

FRIDAY, SEPTEMBER 6

J ack, Charlie and I walked into Mike Armstrong's office at 9:00 a.m. sharp on Friday. He'd been reluctant to meet with us, but when I told him I had something important he needed to see, he finally relented.

His office was a pig sty. It was dusty, there were boxes and files piled haphazardly all over the room. Nothing hung from the eggshell white walls, not even a law degree. The place smelled of stale coffee and there was an almost nauseating aroma emanating from a trash can next to his desk. It had to be some kind of rotting animal flesh. Unfinished chicken he'd eaten at his desk and thrown away, maybe? Whatever it was, I had to say something about it.

"Something's dead in here," I said after I introduced Jack and Charlie and we all sat down.

"Really? What do you mean?"

"Do you have a problem with your sense of smell?" I said.

"I have a condition called congenital anosmia. I was born without a sense of smell. That's why I look like I'm starving to death. I can't smell, so food doesn't have the same taste for me that it does for others. I just don't enjoy it."

"I think you didn't enjoy some chicken or fish or cat food and you tossed it in that can," I said. "Can I get it out of here?"

"Sure, go ahead if it bothers you," Armstrong said.

I picked the can up and took it out to his secretary.

"This stinks to high heaven," I said.

"I'm his secretary, not his maid," she said.

"Would you mind, please? We're trying to have a meeting."

She gave me the stink eye, one that matched the odor emanating from the trash can, and jerked the can out of my hand. She plugged her nose and strutted away.

I walked back in and sat down. Armstrong had a mole on his forehead that was extremely distracting, he was butt ugly, a totally unattractive political candidate, and yet somehow, he'd managed to get the county commission to appoint him to finish out Tanner Jarrett's term when Tanner resigned and moved to Washington. I didn't get it, but when it came to the behind-closed-doors workings of the Washington County Commission, a lot of things didn't make sense.

"I don't have much time," Armstrong said.

"I'm sure you're busy," I said. "This won't take long."

I asked Jack to take out his phone and play the video of Sheila Self's arrival at the party, her performance, and her premature exit.

"You're about to play me a video?" Armstrong said.

"It was taken by a witness who was at the party."

"You won't get it in if we go to trial," he said.

"Why? The witness is willing to testify to what she saw and that she took the video herself. She'll authenticate it. It's admissible and it blows your entire case out of the water."

"I don't want to see it," Armstrong said.

"Why not?" I said. "Don't you want to know what really happened?"

"I know what happened. I have a statement from my victim. We'll soon have DNA evidence to back up her story."

True to form, that made me angry, and when I became angry, I wasn't particularly given to diplomacy. I leaned forward and pointed at him.

"You've screwed up is what you've done. You've been running around talking to every reporter in the country, you've been on television, on the radio, in papers and magazines, and you've backed yourself into a corner. You don't give a damn about the truth at this point. This is about saving face, getting these boys convicted, and getting yourself elected so you can feed at the taxpayer's trough for another eight years."

"Get out," Armstrong said. "All three of you, get out of my office. Now."

I stood and looked at Jack and Charlie. They both seemed calm, but I could tell they were also confused and angry.

"If you don't stop this charade, you're going to wind up facing the ethics board," I said. "I won't call them, but somebody will. What I'm going to do is blow your case up and I'm going to make sure everybody knows what you and your skinhead investigator are doing."

He covered his ears with his hands. I couldn't believe it. He actually put his hands over his ears like a five-year-old.

"Are you kidding me?" I said. "What's wrong with you?"

Next, he started singing, "Get out, get out, get out, get out, get out," to the tune of "Heigh Ho" from "Snow White and the Seven Dwarfs." It was one of the most bizarre displays of behavior I'd ever seen from a district attorney. Hell, it was one of the most bizarre displays of behavior I'd ever seen from anyone.

"Let's go," I said to Jack and Charlie. "This guy has obviously lost his mind."

FRIDAY, SEPTEMBER 27

The storm had died down a bit while everyone waited for the results of the DNA testing to come back from the TBI lab in Knoxville. Armstrong had stopped giving interviews, the two games had been forfeited, and the three players who lived in the house where the party was thrown – including Kevin Davidson – had been dismissed from the football team. Kevin was devastated by the dismissal. He and his parents had come to me asking if there was anything they could do about it, but sadly, there wasn't. He controlled the house where a party was thrown and a stripper had been paid. It was grounds for dismissal from the team. They probably could have tossed him out of school, too, but they didn't.

It was early on a Friday morning and I'd just arrived at the office. I was just sitting down at my desk when our secretary, Beverly Snyder's, voice came over the intercom.

"You have a call from a TBI agent named Anita White on line one," Beverly said.

"Thanks," I said, and I punched the button on the phone.

"Special Agent White," I said. "Always nice to hear from you."

I'd known Anita White for several years. She was an agent in the Johnson City office when I was working as an assistant district attorney and she single-handedly brought down a man who had murdered a judge named Leonard Green. She'd since moved her way up the chain and was now the Assistant Special Agent In Charge of the TBI's Knoxville office. Assistant Special Agent In Charge. The TBI loved their titles.

"How are you, Joe?"

"Hanging in there."

"Caroline?"

"Doing the same. Tough as ever."

"I have some good news and some bad news for you," she said.

"Good news first," I said.

"The lab has been working around the clock on the DNA analysis. They finished yesterday. The woman who made the accusations had DNA from five different males on her and in her."

"How can that possibly be good news?" I said.

"None of the males were ETSU football players. Not a single player sample matched up with anything from the rape kit."

A smile came over my face.

"That's good to hear, Anita. I really appreciate you letting me know. When is the public going to hear about this?"

"We're going to hold a press conference at ETSU on Monday," she said.

"So, this entire thing was a hoax. I wonder if Armstrong will charge her with making a false report."

"I don't think that's going to happen," she said.

"Why not?"

"Because I called Mike Armstrong yesterday afternoon after the report hit my desk. He wasn't pleased at all. He said he's going to do two things: hire a private lab to go over the DNA again and arrest three of the players who were apparently picked out of a lineup by the victim. He's going to announce at the press conference that he is proceeding with the prosecution."

"You're kidding me," I said. "He's actually going to arrest them?"

"He's going to indict them first so he doesn't have to subject his case and his victim to cross-examination during a preliminary hearing."

"I swear, Anita, I can't, for the life of me, figure out what is going on in that man's mind."

"He said he's going to do it the old-fashioned way. He's going to put his pretty young white girl on the stand and have her tell the jury she was raped by three black men. He said he has some other tricks up his sleeve, but he didn't say what they were and I didn't ask."

"He's gone nuts," I said. "We have a video showing the rape couldn't have happened. We went to Mike's office and he wouldn't look at it. When I tried to talk to him, he covered his ears."

"Covered his ears? You mean like a kid?"

"Yeah, can you believe that? Then he started singing some stupid song until we left. It was surreal."

"Well, I'm glad it's your problem," Anita said. "I just thought I'd give you a heads up."

"Thank you, Anita. Nice talking with you."

I hung up the phone and walked into Jack's office. He was working on a motion to exclude some evidence in a DUI case he was handling. Charlie was in court in Elizabethton, about twenty miles away.

"The DNA tests are in. All of the players are clean," I said when I stepped inside Jack's door.

"That's great!" he said. "Absolutely fantastic. Kevin's out of the woods."

"No, I'm afraid he isn't. Anita White just called me. She said they're holding a press conference at ETSU on Monday to make the DNA results public, but Armstrong is also going to announce that he's going to proceed with the prosecution and indict three players who were identified by the victim."

"What? Do you think he can get an indictment?"

"Of course he can. The grand jury will only hear from one witness, and that witness will be Johnson City Police Investigator Bo Riddle. They'll ask him a few questions, he'll tell them a few lies, and they'll rubber stamp a true bill. The old saying that a DA can indict a ham sandwich if he wants to is true."

"So what do we do?"

"Right now? You're going to call Stony and tell her I need to see her again, ASAP. I'm going to call Kevin and his parents and give them the bad news."

FRIDAY, SEPTEMBER 27

"**I** need to get to the bottom of this," I said to Stony. Jack had called her and she'd come to the office within two hours. I was meeting with her alone in the conference room. I didn't want anyone to hear what I was going to ask of her. "It just doesn't make any sense. Somebody, somewhere is calling the shots."

"You don't just think it's a rogue DA showing himself to be tough on crime so he can get re-elected?" she said.

"This goes beyond rogue and passes into the realm of magical realism. I can't think of a single reason Mike Armstrong would want to take up this fight."

"Maybe he and Riddle are both racists. Maybe they don't care. Maybe they just want to inflame an already intense situation."

"And start a race war here in town? Because with the climate in the country today, I can see it happening. I'm afraid people will get killed, maybe lots of people. Why would they want to do that?"

"I think you might be overreacting," Stony said.

"Maybe so, but he's about to arrest three young black men and charge them with raping a woman with no evidence other than the false claims she's making. Unless he manufactures something. A TBI agent told me this morning that he's going to hire a private lab to go over the DNA evidence again because there wasn't a single bit of DNA from an ETSU football player in or on this so-called victim."

"So, the report is done?" Stony said.

"Yeah, they're going to release the results Monday at a press conference. They're also going to indict the three players she picked out of the bogus lineup you told me about. I'm going to need that tape if you can get it."

Stony nodded. "I can."

"That'd be nice," I said. "I need to ask you a favor, Stony. I don't know if you'll want to do it, but if you can, I'd really appreciate it."

"What's the favor?"

"Can you get me some deep intelligence on Armstrong?" I said.

Stony's eyebrows raised. "Deep intelligence? I'm assuming you want me to black bag him."

The FBI's infamous black bag teams were surveillance experts. They could get into and out of places without being noticed, insert listening devices, video cameras, track vehicles, wiretap landline phones and intercept cell phone conversations. They gathered mountains of information without the target ever knowing.

"It's something you're capable of doing," I said. "When we first met, you told me you were an expert in surveillance and had carried out several black bag operations during your career with the FBI."

"I did those jobs after obtaining warrants from federal magistrates or judges."

"I'm afraid we don't have that luxury. If you don't want to do it, I understand. But if you do, I think it could go a long way toward helping us understand what's going on. It might save a few lives. It might save more than a few."

"You're asking me to break the law, Joe."

"You know something, Stony? You did more than twenty years with the FBI, right? I've been at this for more than twenty years now. One thing I've learned is that when you're dealing with the law and this fleeting concept we call justice, exceptions sometimes have to be made. Lines sometimes have to be crossed to ultimately get what we all want, and that's for the right thing to happen. The truth to be discovered. The guilty punished and the innocent freed. I don't believe for a second that you could sit here and look me in the eye and tell me you've never crossed a line that you thought you maybe shouldn't cross."

Stony laced her fingers beneath her chin and began rocking back and forth in the chair. She was on a brief tour of her own soul, searching for something she could live with.

"It'll take me some time to get everything together, get his routines locked in, and get the equipment in place. Then we'll have to wait and see what, if anything comes of it. I'll have to monitor the devices personally. Do you want his office, too?"

"You can do that?"

"I can do anything. They called me Cat Burglar in the unit."

"By all means. Get his office."

"It's going to be expensive."

"The Davidsons will be paying. If they can't, I will."

"Okay," she said. "You've talked me into becoming a criminal. Let's hope it's for the greater good."

Shortly after Stony left, a courier arrived with the report from the independent lab we'd hired to analyze the blood taken from Sheila Self the night she was at the hospital. As soon as I read it, I scanned it and emailed it to Dr. William Kershaw, a forensic toxicologist who was on the faculty at the Quillen College of Medicine and who had testified as an expert witness in dozens of cases in and around Washington County, most often on behalf of the state. I wrote him a brief synopsis of the case and asked if I could call him as soon as possible. I was surprised when I received an email from him only fifteen minutes later. He told me to go ahead and give him a call.

"This is quite interesting," he said when I got him on the phone.

"I thought so, that's why I sent it to you. I'm not sure what the numbers mean, though," I said.

"They mean this woman was still severely impaired when the blood was taken. What concerns me the most about it is the amount of GHB in her system."

"What concerns you about it?" I said.

"When you combine alcohol, ecstasy and GHB, especially at the levels I'm reading in this report, I wouldn't be the least bit hesitant about going into court and offering an expert opinion that this young woman would not have been able to remember what happened to her at the party. She would have been severely impaired, and most likely would have experienced what we call anterograde amnesia. She's actually lucky she didn't pass out or go into a coma or possibly even die."

"And you would testify to that under oath?"

"I've done it before," he said.

"Consider yourself hired," I said. "Can you write me a report that I can attach to a motion I intend to file in court?"

"Certainly."

"How long will it take you?"

"I can have it to you in a couple of days."

"Excellent. Thank you, Dr. Kershaw. I'll be in touch."

I hung up the phone and pounded the desk.

"Gotcha again," I said out loud. "I'm going to make you look like the fool you are, Mike Armstrong."

WEDNESDAY, OCTOBER 9

I pulled up to the Judicial Center in Jonesborough in a foul mood. The bones in Caroline's legs, especially her knees and hips, were causing her a great deal of pain in spite of all the medication she was taking. She'd developed another urinary tract infection and was semi-delirious. I left her in the hands of a new home health care nurse and wasn't the least bit happy about it.

But I had to be in court at 9:00 a.m. Kevin Davidson, a player named Demonte Wright, and a third player named Evan Belle were being arraigned. They'd been indicted two days earlier by the Washington County Grand Jury, arrested the day before, charged with aggravated kidnapping and aggravated rape, and had spent the night in jail. The magistrate who signed the arrest warrants hadn't set a bail amount, so besides the arraignment, we'd be arguing over bail.

The courtroom was packed with members of the media, and there were at least eight television cameras scattered around. The judge was Gwen Neese, a sixty-year-old, attractive woman who had been a judge for six years and hadn't yet managed to develop what I called "black robe fever." She treated people, including defendants and their attorneys, with dignity and respect, and she knew the law cold, which was refreshing after having dealt with men like Leonard Green and Ivan Glass for so many years. Their IQs were lower than most of the people I defended.

Judge Neese walked into court at 9:00 a.m. sharp as the bailiff called the proceeding to order.

"I'd like to take up the case with the three defendants who have been charged with kidnapping and rape first," she said. "Bring them in."

Four uniformed bailiffs flanked the three young men as they walked into the room. They were wearing the orange jumpsuits provided to inmates at the Washington County Detention Center, and they were handcuffed, shackled and waist-chained. It was the kind of treatment reserved for the worst of the worst, and I thought it was over the top.

"This is ridiculous, your Honor," I said as I walked to the podium where the arraignment would take place. "Would you please order the bailiffs to remove the shackles and waist chains?"

"I take it you're representing one of these defendants," Judge Neese said.

"Kevin Davidson," I said. I reached out and put my hand on Kevin's shoulder. "I'm representing him along with my associates, Jack Dillard and Charleston Story."

Jack and Charlie were sitting in the jury box with several other attorneys. The judge looked over at them and nodded. She turned back to me.

"Courtroom security decisions are made by the sheriff's department, Mr. Dillard. You know that. These men are all charged with two Class A felonies. I can't speak for the sheriff or whoever made the decision about the waist chains and shackles, but I would imagine it's just standard operating procedure for these charges."

"The charges are completely baseless," I said. "There isn't enough evidence to have probable cause for an arrest."

"The grand jury obviously disagreed with your assessment," the judge said.

"You and I both know how grand juries work. They hear one side and they rubber stamp what the prosecution puts in front of them."

Mike Armstrong was sitting at the prosecution table. He stood quickly.

"I take offense to that remark," Armstrong said. "We've investigated this case thoroughly, we have a positive identification from the victim, and we intend to hold these men accountable for the serious crimes they committed."

"I tried to show Mr. Armstrong a video we obtained that was taken at the party where my client and his teammates allegedly kidnapped and raped this so-called victim. It clearly shows that none of what she is saying is true. Mr. Armstrong refused to look at the video. When I tried to talk to him, he covered his ears like a child and wouldn't listen to anything I had to say. The line-up that produced the identification of which Mr. Armstrong speaks was illegal. Totally bogus. And we can prove it. On top of that, we have an expert who will testify that the alleged victim had such a high concentration of drugs in her system – one in particular called gamma hydroxybutyrate – that she wouldn't have been able to remember what happened the night this alleged assault took place."

"And I'll cross-examine this so-called expert and discredit him in front of the jury," Armstrong said.

"That'll be interesting, since he's testified for the state dozens of times," I said.

"Gentlemen, please. We're not here to try the case," the judge said. "We're here for arraignment."

"I realize that," I said. "I just want the court to be aware that this case has been brought on the flimsiest evidence I've seen in my entire career. I have no idea why, but I'll eventually get to the bottom of it. And when I do, there will be severe ramifications."

"Excuse me," Armstrong said. "Did Mr. Dillard just make some kind of veiled threat?"

I turned and looked at him.

"You're going to pay for what you're doing to these young men, you and that goon that's helping you. That's not a veiled threat. It's a promise."

"That's enough," Judge Neese said.

"Every one of these young men voluntarily gave DNA samples to the police, your Honor," I said. "When the results of the testing came back from the TBI lab, there wasn't a trace of DNA from any of them on or in the victim, who just happens to be a stripper and a prostitute. And Mr. Armstrong's investigator, Bo Riddle, assaulted my client during his first interview. He kneed him in the testicles."

"That's an outrageous accusation!" Armstrong bellowed.

Judge Neese banged her gavel hard. It was the first time I'd ever seen her use the gavel.

"I said that's *enough*," she said sternly. "Let's keep it civil. Mr. Dillard, do you waive the reading of the formal indictment?"

"We do."

"How does your client plead?"

"Not guilty. Totally innocent. Railroaded."

"Please don't force me to hold you in contempt," Judge Neese said.

"I'm sorry, your Honor. I'm angry about this one."

"As you well know, there is no place for anger in a courtroom. You're a respected and experienced attorney, Mr. Dillard. Frankly, I'm surprised you'd behave in such a manner."

"You'll understand my feelings more as this case proceeds," I said. "At some point, I hope you'll share my anger and put a stop to this charade."

"You need to hold him in contempt, judge," Armstrong said. "He keeps insulting the district attorney general's office, the grand jury, the entire system."

I wanted to tell Armstrong that I held *him* in contempt, but I'd pushed the envelope far enough. I'd walked in there wanting to make an impression on Judge Neese. I wanted to make sure she knew I was upset, that I thought Kevin Davidson and his friends were being railroaded, and that something very wrong was going on with the district attorney general. I knew Judge Neese respected me. I'd known her for a long, long time. I knew her when she was a practicing attorney. I remembered when she got drunk and flashed her breasts at a raucous

Christmas party many years earlier. I felt like I'd gotten her attention, and that she understood how strongly I felt about Kevin's innocence. Mission accomplished. She would listen to me going forward.

"Mr. Demonte Wright," the judge said. "Please step forward to the microphone."

Demonte, a linebacker who had long dreadlocks and looked like he'd been carved from granite, shuffled forward.

"Have you spoken to an attorney, sir?" the judge said.

"I can't afford a lawyer," he said.

"What about you, Mr. Belle?" the judge said.

Evan Belle moved forward. His hair was long and unruly. He looked at the floor as he spoke.

"I can't afford a lawyer, either," he said.

Judge Neese turned to her clerk, was handed a couple of sheets of paper, and handed the papers to the bailiffs.

"I need both of you to fill these out," she said. "They're affidavits of indigency. List your assets and your debts and be truthful about it. If I find you're unable to pay for a lawyer, I'll appoint lawyers to represent you."

"Can we talk about bail?" I said when the other two players shuffled over to a table at the side of the courtroom to fill out their forms.

"The state opposes bail," Armstrong said.

"Of course you do," I said, "but unfortunately for you, they're entitled to a bail. This isn't a capital murder case. My client was at the top of his class and has been accepted to law school, your Honor. Unfortunately, now that he's been charged, ETSU will undoubtedly kick him out of school and his future in law school is threatened. He isn't a flight risk. The case against him is as weak as any I've ever seen. His mother and father are paying his legal fees, which will more than likely be substantial if the case goes to trial. I'm just asking for a reasonable amount of bond so he doesn't have to sit in jail while this plays out and so his parents aren't forced into bankruptcy. I don't represent the others who have been charged, but the case against them is as weak as the case against Mr. Davidson."

"Mr. Armstrong?" the judge said.

"If you're going to set a bail, the state asks for at least a half-million dollars," he said.

"Totally unreasonable," I said.

"Bond is set at seventy-five thousand dollars per defendant, cash or corporate surety," the judge said.

"Does that mean I have to pay seventy-five thousand dollars to get out of jail?" Kevin whispered in my ear.

"No. You call a bail bondsman. He'll charge you ten percent. It'll cost your parents seventy-five hundred to get you out."

"This is ridiculous," he whispered.

"I'm sorry. It's the best we can do for now."

The other two players filled out their forms and passed them up to the judge. She looked them over and said, "All right, having reviewed these affidavits, I find both defendants to be indigent. Mr. Wright, I'm going to appoint the public defender's office to represent you."

Patrick Lonon, a long-time public defender, stepped to the podium. The judge looked over at the jury box.

"Mr. Beaumont, would you be willing to represent Mr. Belle?" the judge said.

"Happy to," Jim Beaumont said, and he walked to the podium. Beaumont had been practicing law for more than forty years in the First Judicial District. He dressed like a cowboy, his mouth was covered by a long, white moustache and goatee, and he spoke in a deep, throaty Southern drawl. He was an excellent lawyer, and I was glad to have him on our side.

Both Demonte Wright and Evan Belle waived the reading of the indictment and entered pleas of not guilty.

"Bail is set at seventy-five thousand dollars for both of these defendants," Judge Neese said. "What about scheduling?"

The lawyers all looked at each other. I decided to speak up.

"Set it for trial as soon as you possibly can, please," I said.

"We're still developing evidence and witnesses," Armstrong said. "We'll need at least six months."

"If you're still developing witnesses, you should have held off on indicting them," Judge Neese said.

She looked through her calendar, conferred with her clerk, and said, "December tenth. Two months and one day from today. The deadlines for motions, experts, alibis, and discovery will be tight. I'll send all of you a scheduling order. I suggest you get to work."

I asked one of the bailiffs if I could speak to my client in the jury room before they returned him to the holding cell in back, and he agreed. He stood outside as I closed the door.

"Take a seat," I said to Kevin.

His eyes were down and his shoulders slumped. When he raised his eyes to look at me, they were glistening with tears.

"Why are they doing this to me?" he said. "Everything I've worked so hard for is gone. I guarantee you the paperwork has already been signed to kick me out of school. I'll get a notice soon from UT's law school that my acceptance has been rescinded. And for what? Because I was stupid enough to let a stripper come into our house at a party. That's all I did. I didn't lay a hand on her."

"I know," I said, sitting down next to him. "I believe you. Right now, though, I'm concerned about your safety. Where are you planning to go when your parents get you out of jail?"

He shook his head slowly.

"I don't know. I won't be able to move back into the house if they kick me out of school. I was surprised they didn't make us leave when they kicked us off the team, but nobody told us to go. They'll tell me to go now, for sure. I guess maybe I could get a job and rent a place somewhere around here until this is over. I doubt it, though. Nobody will give me a job after all this publicity."

"Maybe you should think about going to Collierville and staying with your parents."

"Why? I don't want to move back in with my parents. Besides, it's six hundred miles away. I'd like to stay closer, maybe try to help out somehow."

"I'm afraid somebody will try to hurt you," I said. "A lot of bitterness and hatred has come boiling to the surface in the country over the past couple of years. You're a black man accused of raping a white woman. This case has received national publicity. I think you're going to have to be extremely careful."

"What are they going to do to me that hasn't already been done? Kill me? Dying would be better than this."

"If you don't want to go home, why don't you come stay with my wife and me? She's pretty sick right now, but you can help me out with her if you don't mind. You can help out at the law office some if you want. Help us out with your case. I'd feel a lot better knowing you're safe."

"Really?" Kevin said. "You'd do that for me?"

"Yeah, and I don't even have to ask my wife, because I know what her answer would be. She'd say, 'If he needs a place to stay, if he needs help, we'll help him.'"

"You're a good man," he said.

"You don't know me that well. But I expect you to pay it forward someday."

"Mr. Dillard, am I going to spend the rest of my life in jail?"

"No. I'm not going to let that happen. But you're in for a hard, hard ride over the next few months. You'll have to be braver and tougher than you've ever been. Bad things happen to good people, Kevin. My wife has had cancer for years, but she fights through the pain every day because she wants to live. I want the same thing for you. I want you to live. But you have to want it, too. You can't give in to despair. Do you think your parents will be okay with you staying with me?"

"I think they'll be okay with it."

"Good. There's only one problem we have to deal with."

"What's that?"

"You have to make friends with the guardian of the property at my house."

He looked at me curiously.

"He's a German shepherd. His name is Rio. If he likes you, and I think he will, nobody will get anywhere near you."

WEDNESDAY, OCTOBER 9

Kevin Davidson had lunch with his parents after they bailed him out of jail. They called me while they were still all at the restaurant. I was apparently on speaker while we talked. They must have been outside because I could hear the wind whistling lightly over the phone.

"Can you guarantee his safety?" Mr. Davidson asked me.

I had returned home to find Caroline doing better after receiving some pain meds and a thousand milliliters of sodium chloride through an intravenous drip. I'd asked her about Kevin staying with us, and her response was, "Of course," just like I knew it would be.

"There aren't any guarantees," I said to Mr. Davidson. "We live out in the county, on a bluff that overlooks the lake. We don't have any neighbors we can see or hear. I have a German shepherd who is extremely territorial and I have weapons in my house that I know how to use. In fact, I wouldn't hesitate to use them to protect your son. But I can't watch him every minute of every day. I'm sure he'll have places he wants to go occasionally just to keep from going stir crazy. I'll do all I can, but honestly, no, I can't absolutely guarantee his safety. The only way to do that would be for him to disappear until the trial. He'd have to go into hiding. That might be something you want to consider."

"But he hasn't done anything wrong!" Mr. Davidson yelled.

"I understand that, but for whatever reason, he's been accused. Racial tensions are extremely high. They were high before this happened. Kevin will be a target for white supremacists, white nationalists, neo-Nazis, all of those groups. I feel sure there are some who would want to make an example of him."

"You said you know how to use the weapons you have," Mr. Davidson said. "Do you mind if I ask what kind of weapons are in your home?"

"Dangerous weapons. The kind that can kill people from close range or long range."

"Do you have a military background, Mr. Dillard?"

"I was a US Army Ranger when I was young."

"Did you see combat?"

"I did."

"Have you ever killed anyone?"

"These are extremely personal questions, Mr. Davidson."

"If I'm going to put my son's life in your hands, I want to know. Have you ever killed anyone?"

"I have."

"How many?"

"More than I care to admit."

"I don't want to send him into hiding like a coward, especially since he's done nothing wrong," Mr. Davidson said, "and from what you've told me, I think you can do a better job of protecting him than I can. I have no military background; I'm not some kind of bad ass. I don't even own a gun. I'd feel better if he stays with you."

"Fine," I said. "I tell you what. Kevin has his own car, right?"

"I don't know if you'd call it a car, but it has four wheels and occasionally gets him from place to place," Mr. Davidson said.

"What time are you planning to go to Kevin's house and pick up his things?"

"We were going to go as soon as we're finished here."

"Give me an hour. I'll get my son to drive me to Johnson City and I'll meet you guys at Kevin's house. We'll load up his things and he can follow us out here to my house. I'll make sure we're not tailed. No one will know he's here, at least for a while. Someone will most likely find out eventually."

We hung up and I called Jack. He agreed to come and pick me up and take me to Johnson City. When he showed up, I kissed Caroline and told her I'd return with our new house guest in a couple of hours. I climbed into Jack's Jeep, and the first thing he said was, "Are you sure this is a good idea, Dad?"

"No. Not at all. I'm just trying to do what's best for Kevin."

"Some crackpot might try to kill him."

"That's the whole point of him coming to our place, Jack. You remember a few years back when that sick coward John Lipscomb killed three of Erlene Barlowe's girls out on the lake and then wound up sending a group of *sicarios* from Columbia to kill me and our entire family?"

"How could I forget it? You took us to Michigan and made us stay there with your old Army buddy until it was over."

"The point is that the house is defensible. If someone were to come, Rio would let me know. I have a pretty nice little cache of weapons. I can still shoot."

"But why would you want to take that risk?"

I turned and looked him in the eye.

"You're my son. Do I even have to answer that question?"

He shook his head and turned back to the road.

"You're doing the right thing," he said. "Living up to your very ridiculously high moral code."

"That's right. And it's a code you share, or at least I hope you do. I just feel like this is what I should do. And maybe I'm over thinking it. Maybe nobody will bother Kevin."

"I hope not," Jack said. "But if they do, I want to be there, too."

Jack was as good with many of the weapons as I was. I'd taken him shooting with me hundreds of times over the years. But he'd never been in combat. He'd been in his share of fistfights, but fistfights and firefights are two entirely different animals. He'd wanted to enlist after he graduated from law school, but I'd talked him out of it. I just couldn't bear the thought of him putting himself in harm's way so the military industrial complex that had come to dominate our government and our foreign policy could continue to feed itself. It was feeding itself just fine without him. In fact, it was downright bloated. The budget for the U.S. military was more than $825 billion and there were active duty U.S. military personnel in roughly one hundred and sixty countries around the world. It was completely out of control, accompanied by one of the most masterful marketing campaigns ever devised. When I got out of the service, nobody noticed. Now, every soldier was a hero until they came home and tried to get help from the Veterans Administration. The VA was a bureaucratic mess. Congress had been bought by the defense industry, and it wasn't going to change anytime soon. Jack finally agreed that he could do more good at home than somewhere in the Middle East, where he had a far better chance of losing a limb or winding up in a body bag than making some kind of meaningful difference.

When we pulled alongside the curb in front of Kevin's house, there was a Johnson City Police Department cruiser sitting in front of us. There were several cars nearby, both in the driveway and on the street. Jack and I went up and knocked on the door. It was opened by a Johnson City officer named David Milhorn. He was a young guy, thick and muscular like Jack. I'd seen him in court a couple of times, but I didn't know anything about him other than he was inexperienced, maybe even still a rookie.

"Can I help you?" he said.

"I'm Joe Dillard, Kevin Davidson's lawyer."

"So?"

"I'm here to help him move out."

"I don't think you should come in," he said.

"Get out of my way," I said, and I shouldered past him. I stepped into the house and said "Kevin! It's Joe Dillard."

"Stop right where you are." The voice came from behind me. I turned to see Officer Milhorn pointing a taser gun at me.

"You intend to use that, do you, Officer Milhorn?" I said.

"I told you not to come in."

"No, you didn't. You said, 'I don't think you should come in,' but this isn't your property. You don't control it. Until Kevin walks out the door, he controls it and he invited me. Now put that thing away before you get yourself sued and lose your job."

"Who do you think you are?" Milhorn said. "You can't just disobey a police officer."

"You're wrong about that," I said. "There's no law that says I have to obey police officers, especially when the police officer is young, out of line, and full of shit."

About this time, Kevin and his parents came through a doorway and into the room.

"Good, now I have witnesses," I said. "Kevin, do I have your permission to be here?"

"Yes, sir."

"You and your parents invited me, didn't you?"

"Yes, we did."

I stared at Milhorn. I could almost see his mind working, trying to decide what to do.

"Just put it away," I said. "We'll chalk it up to a rookie mistake and move on. No hard feelings. I'm only here to help Kevin move out."

He finally lowered the taser and I felt a pang of relief. I had no desire to be zapped by fifty thousand volts of electricity.

"Why would a lawyer come help his client move out of a place?" Milhorn said.

"None of your business. Why are you even here, Officer Milhorn? Do you have reason to believe a crime is being committed?"

"I was ordered by my watch commander to post here until your client came and moved out. I believe the university called and asked for police assistance. I've been instructed to get his keys and make sure he doesn't do any damage."

"Fine. Just let us do what we came to do. We'll be out of here shortly."

Officer Milhorn stood by the door while the rest of us went to work. College athletes, like most college students, live like gypsies. They travel light and can be ready to move at a moment's notice. Kevin had the basics: a small television, a laptop, and his clothing. His parents put the television and some of his clothing in their car, and Kevin put the rest of his clothes, his toiletries, a guitar, and some photographs in his car. We were loaded up and out of there in thirty minutes. Nobody bothered to say goodbye to Officer Milhorn.

Less than two minutes after we got into the car and drove away, Jack said, "You're a complete lunatic, you know that?"

"What? I'm not going to let some snot-nosed rookie cop boss me around. They intimidate people all the time, Jack, because they have a badge and a gun. They think they can tell people what to do and they have to do it automatically. It doesn't work that way. I was telling him the truth. There is no law that says you have to do something just because a cop tells you to. If a cop gives you a lawful, reasonable order, then you have to comply. If they're just bullying you, you can tell them to piss up a rope."

"He almost tasered you, Dad."

"Would have been a terrible mistake for him, and to his credit, he finally realized it."

"I'll be glad when I have your confidence," Jack said.

"Thanks. Me, too."

"But I'll never be as crazy as you are. Never."

WEDNESDAY, OCTOBER 9

Investigator Bo Riddle had called the watch commander early in the afternoon to see if he'd heard anything about where Kevin Davidson had gone after he was released from jail. Riddle knew he'd been banished from his home by the university and kicked out of school. He wanted to know where Davidson was going, because he and his friends had plans, the kind of plans he didn't wish to discuss with the watch commander.

The watch commander had told Riddle he'd assigned a rookie named David Milhorn to "supervise" the removal of Kevin Davidson's belongings from the home and to confiscate his keys. The watch commander also said Milhorn reported that Davidson had showed up along with his parents and his lawyer, gathered his belongings, surrendered his keys, and left.

Riddle asked for Milhorn's cell number and the watch commander gave it to him. He dialed it immediately.

"David Milhorn," a voice said.

"Officer Milhorn, this is Investigator Bo Riddle. I'm lead on the ETSU rape case, and I understand you were at Kevin Davidson's house today when he came and picked up his things."

"That's right," Milhorn said.

"So everything went smoothly?"

"Yeah, it was fine, except for the lawyer. I almost tased him."

"Tased him? Why?"

"Because he was a belligerent bastard. I told him he couldn't come in the house and he just barged right past me. I didn't take it well."

"His lawyer's a jackass. All defense lawyers are jackasses," Riddle said. "How did it turn out?"

"It was tense for a minute, but I eventually let him come inside. They gathered up the kid's things and left."

"Who's they?" Riddle said.

"The kid, his parents and the lawyer and the lawyer's son."

"Did you hear any of them say anything about where the kid was going?"

"I got the impression he was going to stay with his lawyer."

"Seriously? The kid has an old Honda registered in his name. Was he driving it?"

"Yeah."

"When they left, did you notice if the kid followed the parents or the lawyer?"

"I noticed. The parents went west, and the lawyer's son, who was driving a Jeep, went east. The lawyer was riding with his son. The kid followed the Jeep."

"Thanks," Riddle said. "Just trying to stay on top of things for my investigation. Appreciate your help."

Riddle disconnected the phone, wondering exactly what was going on. The kid had no girlfriend that Riddle knew of. He had no family in the area. Riddle wondered if Dillard really had decided to take him in until the trial.

Part of him hoped exactly that. Dillard was already a marked man simply by virtue of representing a nigger who had raped a white woman. If he was housing him and protecting him as well, bad things were in store for Joe Dillard.

WEDNESDAY, OCTOBER 9

The introduction to Rio had gone well; the dog sniffed him over, licked his hand, and wandered away.

"Okay," I said. "You've passed inspection. You're in. He'll still bark at you when you come to the front door. Just unlock it and talk to him. He'll calm down and let you in. We'll play a little game tonight with him that will really make him like you."

I invited Jack and Charlie over for supper. Caroline had put a pot roast in the slow cooker, and Caroline, Kevin, Jack, Charlie and I all sat down for supper. I wanted to make Kevin feel as comfortable as possible. We ate and made small talk, and after we were finished eating, I helped Caroline and Charlie clean up while Jack helped Kevin get settled into Jack's old room, showed him which television remote operated which function, and familiarized him with the bathroom and the inside of the house. Afterward, I took him outside and introduced him to Sadie, Charlie's horse, and showed him around the barn and the property. I showed him the trail where I still jogged almost every morning at 5:30 or 6:00 a.m., and I showed him the boundaries of the ten acres we owned. We stood looking down onto the lake, which the Tennessee Valley Authority had drawn down more than ten feet since Labor Day. The government agency constantly manipulated the water levels by using a system of dams.

"It's beautiful up here," Kevin said.

"Yeah. I love it. We've been here a long time."

"Can I ask you a question, Mr. Dillard?" Kevin said.

"Sure. Fire away."

"Why are you doing this? Why are you taking me in, giving me a job? You could be putting yourself at risk."

"I'm not afraid for me," I said. "I'm afraid for you. I'll just be honest with you, Kevin. You're the only player who's going to be out on bond before the trial. The others can't afford it. They'll sit in jail until the trial. I think they'll be safe there, because the sheriff runs a tight ship at the jail. But since you're out, you'll be the target. I think some white supremacist looking to make a name for himself could try to kill you, and I want to do everything in my power to make certain that doesn't happen."

"But why do you care?" he said.

"Because I'm a human being. Because I'm a lawyer. Because I look at this case and it stinks to high heaven. They don't have any reliable evidence against you, but they indicted you anyway. The DNA tests came back negative. The photo lineup Bo Riddle showed the girl was coached, unconstitutional, and will never see the inside of a courtroom. We have video of everything that happened from the time the girl arrived at the party until the time she left. It proves no rape took place, but Mike Armstrong wouldn't even look at it."

"So you think this is purely a racial thing?" Kevin said.

"That's part of it, especially with Riddle, but there's something else going on I haven't been able to figure out. I'll let you know as soon as I do."

Kevin turned to face me and stuck out his hand.

"Thank you, Mr. Dillard. I mean it. Right now, I feel like my entire world has been blown apart, but there's something about you that makes me think it's going to turn out all right."

"I hope so, Kevin," I said. "I really do."

We went back inside when it grew dark.

"Let's play that game I was talking about," I said.

I walked into the den and picked up a tennis ball that I kept on a shelf near the door. Rio immediately started whining, his tail banging into a coffee table.

"Sit," I said, and the dog sat.

"Stay."

I handed the ball to Kevin.

"Walk out onto the deck, close the door, and throw the ball in any direction you want," I said. "Don't throw it too hard toward the lake or it might roll over the bluff. After you throw it, open the door and let Rio out."

Rio whined while Kevin went out, but he stayed where he was. I watched Kevin throw the ball with his left hand. He came back to the door and opened it. Rio looked at me.

"Go get it," I said, and he shot through the door like a rocket.

"Less than five minutes, guaranteed," I said.

About four minutes later, the dog was back with the ball in his mouth. He dropped it at Kevin's feet.

"That means do it again," I said, so Kevin repeated the whole process. He even gave Rio the "sit" and "stay" commands. I watched while they played the game for a half-hour or so.

"Okay," I said after Kevin had thrown the ball and Rio had retrieved it seven or eight times, "that's enough for tonight. Kevin, you've made a lifelong friend."

We spent the rest of the evening watching the National League Division Series on television. The game ran pretty late. Jack and Charlie left around 10:00 p.m., and Caroline went to bed thirty minutes before. The ballgame was a blowout, and at some point I turned to Kevin and said, "Kevin, I played ball in high school with black guys and I served with black guys in the Army. I sweated and trained with them, drank beer with them, shared food with them, even fought in combat alongside them. I've represented dozens of black men and women over my career. But you know what? I never thought to ask one of them what it's like to be black in the United States of America. So I'm going to ask you. What's it like?"

He paused, considering his answer. That was something I'd noticed about Kevin. He was thoughtful in his approach to questions like the one I had just posed. He didn't just blurt out the first thing that came to his mind.

"It's hard for me to speak for so many," he began, "because my life has been different than the lives of a lot of young blacks in this country. My father was always around. He was a steady influence, a good man. My mother was the same. Hard-working, conscientious, intelligent and loving. I always had clothes to wear and there was always food on the table. We ate as a family every evening, even if I was practicing and didn't get home until late. Everyone would wait until we could all eat together. I wasn't running the streets like so many others. I was in a safe, loving environment at home and at school, I worked hard in the classroom and in sports.

"But there have been things that happened – a lot of things – that made me uncomfortable, made me ashamed, made me angry. I'll give you a couple of examples. I was stopped by the police three times my freshman year at Collierville, and all I was doing was walking to class. We had to walk outside from one building to another, and I would get stopped and questioned while my white classmates walked right past me. Why did they stop me and harass me? Because I was wearing red sweatbands. The school colors were red and white. A lot of white guys, especially athletes, wore red sweatbands, but on me, it was taken by the white cops as flashing gang colors. I finally just quit wearing them. After I got my license, I was stopped a half-a-dozen times by the Collierville police, for no other reason than I was a young black man driving around in a nice, predominantly white, neighborhood.

"My parents tried to prepare me, they warned me about some of the things I'd come up against, but it's still hard to take when you're walking down the street and a white woman that's walking towards you crosses the street and clutches her purse. I remember playing spin the bottle at a party with a bunch of white kids from my neighborhood when I was in the sixth grade. I spun the bottle and it pointed at this girl named Susan Dell. I leaned over to kiss her and she got up and ran out of the room. A friend invited me over to swim in his pool when I was sixteen. When his father came home, it was immediately apparent that he was uncomfortable with me being in the pool. He asked my friend to ask me to leave. I know as I got older my mother was afraid every time I left the house because so many young black men were being shot by white police officers, people who were supposed to serve and protect us. You learn to cope with it, but you never really feel free. And you know why? It's because you aren't, not in the true sense of the word. Not in the white sense of the word."

I didn't know what to say. Everything he'd said had a ring of truth to it, and what was worse, here was a kid who had tried his entire life to do everything right, to walk that fine line, to advance and excel in a society where the deck was stacked against him, and now he'd fallen victim to the very things he'd just talked about. It was a perfect storm, and it would certainly devour this young man if I couldn't do something to calm the winds. I decided right then and there I had to do something, and soon. I couldn't let this case run its course through the normal channels. The risk was too great that we could wind up with a jury full of closet racists and that Kevin would go to the penitentiary for the rest of his life.

My biggest problem was that there was no real legal mechanism for walking into Criminal Court and asking a judge to dismiss an indictment based on a lack of evidence. Defense lawyers could challenge indictments on mistakes in the form of the indictment or mistakes in the charges, but even if we managed to get the case tossed on technical defects in the indictment – and there weren't any in Kevin's case – Mike Armstrong would just go back to the grand jury, present his case again, get proper indictments against the players, and we'd start back at square one. What I needed to do was to attack what little evidence they had piece by piece, try to get it all excluded by filing motions in *limine*, get the judge on our side, and then gut Armstrong at trial. A motion in *limine* is a motion filed before the trial, asking the court for an order limiting or preventing the use of certain evidence during the trial.

I decided to get everyone together first thing in the morning and organize the attack. I also decided to do something I normally wouldn't have done, which was to tell the lawyers representing the other two players what I was planning to do. They were both excellent lawyers, and I thought they might be able to offer some help.

"I'm going to hit the hay," I said to Kevin. "I usually get up early and go for a run along a trail that runs through the woods at the top of the bluff above the lake. You're welcome to join me, or you can sleep in."

"What time do you get up?"

"Usually around five," I said. "I hit the trail around six."

"I'll get up and go with you," he said. "Might as well get up and move around. I'll get depressed if I just sit around and worry."

"Good. I'll see you in the morning."

I went back into the bedroom, kissed Caroline on the forehead, and went to sleep.

★★★

They came around three-thirty in the morning, the miserable cowards. It started when I was awakened by a low, steady growl coming from Rio. He was standing beneath the bedroom window, and I rolled out of bed and tried to calm him. What he was doing was extremely unusual. Rio knew the difference between a deer walking through the yard and a threat. Something, or someone, was outside that wasn't supposed to be there. I opened the blinds and looked out the window but couldn't see anything. It was pitch black outside, which was another sign that something was wrong. We had a security light at the corner of the house by the driveway. It had either quit working or someone had disabled it.

I moved quickly to the closet and threw on a dark hoodie, a pair of sweats and my running shoes. Then I grabbed a Remington Model 1100 Tactical shotgun and started sliding twelve-gauge, double-ought buckshot rounds into the magazine. It held eight.

I stepped back into the bedroom and Caroline was sitting up.

"What's going on?" she said.

"I don't know, but something isn't right. The hair on Rio's back is standing straight up."

"What are you going to do?"

"Go out there and see what's going on."

"Why don't you call the police?"

"Go ahead," I said, and she reached over for her phone.

"Stay in here. Keep Rio with you. If I'm not back in five minutes, pick up a weapon and don't be afraid to use it."

Caroline had occasionally enjoyed going along with Jack and I on our shooting jaunts and could handle a variety of weapons. She wasn't a dead-eye, but if a person got close enough, she could put a bullet in them. And I had no doubt she'd do it, too, to protect her home, herself, her dogs, and Kevin Davidson.

I slipped out of the bedroom and closed the door. I decided to go out the back, down the steps off the deck and circle around the house. I moved quickly, the shotgun at my shoulder. Just as I came around the corner of the house, I heard the *rat tat tat* of an assault rifle coming from the road at the top of the driveway. It had the distinctive sound of the Kalashnikov AK-47. The windows in the garage began to break. I huddled against the side of the house. There was no way I could go up against an assault rifle with a shotgun from that distance, and I had no idea how many people with weapons were out there. The firing continued as the shooter began to shred Kevin's car, which was parked just to the side of the driveway on an asphalt pull-off. Finally, the shooting stopped, and the next thing I heard was a loud *whoosh* as flames lit up the night sky. Next came the sound of a diesel engine, most likely a large pick-up, and a male voice that yelled: "Nigger lover!"

I began to run toward the sound of the truck, firing the shotgun as I went. I squeezed off five rounds as the truck roared off into the darkness. I stopped running and moved the rest of the way up the driveway toward the fire. It was just a few feet off the road, and it only took a few seconds for me to realize what they'd done. I stood there staring, with a feeling of surreal bewilderment coming over me.

I'd read about it in books. I'd seen it in the movies.

But never, not once in my life, had I envisioned someone burning a cross in my front yard.

THURSDAY, OCTOBER 10

After I made sure they were gone by doing a sweep around the house and letting Rio out to do his own grid search, I dragged a water hose up and doused the flames. The cross was only about four feet high, made from a four-by-four post and a two-by-four crosspiece that had been nailed together. It was a hasty and sloppy job as far as intimidation tactics go, but I guess it served its purpose. I was certainly on notice that the racists knew where I lived and were willing to show up at my house. I didn't know whether they were aware that Kevin Davidson was sleeping in Jack's room. They hadn't tried to get to him, but the thought nagged at me that someone knew, and I wondered who that person was and how he found out. It had to be a man. Women didn't typically do cross-burnings.

I looked back toward the house to see Kevin walking in my direction.

"Go back inside!" I yelled. "Stay with Caroline! I'll be in soon!"

A Washington County Sheriff's Department deputy named Rocky Littleton showed up at the house about ten minutes after Caroline made her call. I took the shotgun and leaned it against the wall inside the garage and went back out to talk with him. He took some photos and filled out a report.

"You want me to wake up the sheriff?" he said.

"No point. There's nothing he can do tonight."

"You didn't get a look at any of them?"

"No. All I can tell you was it sounded like a diesel pick-up truck."

"Didn't recognize the voice that yelled?"

I shook my head. "Sorry."

"Not much to go on here, Mr. Dillard," Deputy Littleton said. "I'll get forensics to come out and gather up bullets and shell casings. They shot your garage all to hell."

"I know."

"I hope your vehicles are insured."

"They are. So's the house. It'll be okay."

"I have to tell you something," Littleton said. "I admire you for taking this case. A lot of lawyers would have run like their hair was on fire, but you stepped right up, just like you always have. And for what it's worth, from where I'm standing – and this goes for a lot of my buddies at the department – your client is being shafted. A lot of folks at the Johnson City Police Department feel the same way. I hope you can get it straightened out. There are a few racists around, we all know that, but for the most part the people here are good people. This has already made us look bad all over the country, and it just isn't right."

"Thank you," I said. "I appreciate it. Now let me ask you a question. You have some discretion as to whether you make your report public, correct?"

"Yes, sir. It's a bit of a gray area, but if the case is still under investigation, then I don't have to make the report available to the media."

"Is the case still under investigation?" I said.

"Do we know who burned the cross and made Swiss cheese out of your garage door?"

"No, we don't."

"Then as far as I'm concerned, it's still under investigation."

"I appreciate that, Deputy Littleton. I really do. I wasn't looking forward to reading in the paper tomorrow or the next day about what happened here tonight."

"I'll talk to the sheriff in a couple of hours," Littleton said. "He's an early riser. We'll muster up our informants, get some folks out in the streets, see if we can't find out who did this. Somebody will want to take credit. They'll run their mouths. They always do."

"I'm looking forward to meeting them," I said. "Maybe I'll get a chance to return the favor in some way."

FRIDAY, OCTOBER 11

K evin and I skipped our run the next morning for obvious reasons. He was extremely upset about what happened, but I told him we had no idea whether the people who fired shots into the garage and burned the cross knew he was there. Even if they didn't, he was still terrified by what had happened. I understood. Assault rifles and burning crosses. It was a hell of a night.

Sheriff Leon Bates showed up at the house at 6:00 a.m. His forensics people were just finishing up after combing over the garage, Kevin's car, and the area around the cross. They'd also combed both sides of the road leading to my house for a half-mile in each direction. I didn't think they'd found much. They'd removed the blackened cross and put it in a van. It probably wouldn't yield much in the way of evidence, but you never knew.

Leon called my cell when he pulled up outside and I invited him in for a cup of coffee. Caroline was still asleep, and I'd finally talked Kevin into going back to bed. He'd sat at the kitchen table with a stunned look on his face for more than an hour before I managed to persuade him to try to get some more sleep.

Leon walked in, mid-forties, long and lanky. He removed his cowboy hat and sat down at the table.

"Brother Dillard, looks like you've gotten yourself into another fine mess."

"Looks that way," I said. "I seem to be pretty good at fine messes."

"They shot your garage door up pretty bad," Leon said.

"Insurance will cover all the damage to the garage," I said. "Same with Caroline's car and my truck. And Kevin said his parents have insurance on his car."

"When I find these boys, and I promise you I will, they're gonna do a bunch of time if they make it to the jail."

"Don't go killing anybody you don't absolutely have to kill," I said.

I knew Leon wasn't afraid to pull a trigger. He also wasn't above torturing suspects if the stakes were high enough and he needed information immediately. He had his very own black site he called "The Farm" where he sometimes took prisoners for "special" interrogations. He'd used it to get information out of a suspect who was killing judges all over the state almost a year earlier. The judge and his girlfriend were also kidnapping, torturing, raping and killing young women. They were both completely depraved. I was involved in that case, and as much as I hated to admit it, I knew about what Leon had done and was okay with the result. I wasn't particularly comfortable with it, but looking back, it had saved some lives.

"So we're looking at aggravated assault, shooting into an occupied dwelling, misdemeanor vandalism, and a hate crime enhancement at sentencing because of the cross," Leon said. "Deputy Littleton told me you heard one of them yell out 'nigger lover.' That right?"

"Unfortunately."

"Just more evidence for the hate crime enhancement. No idea how many there were?"

"No, but my guess would be three or four. They had to get the hole dug, put the cross in it, douse it with some kind of accelerant, and ignite it. Then there was the trigger man who started blasting away with the assault rifle."

"Say you think it was a diesel pick-up?"

"I'm sure of it. The sound is as distinctive as that AK-47."

"We'll be checking all the security cameras at businesses within a few miles of here. We might get lucky. It happened around three-thirty?"

"Rio woke me up at three-thirty-two. I looked at the clock. They were gone less than ten minutes later."

"Not much traffic on the roads around here that time of night," Leon said. "I hope a diesel truck shows up on a camera close by."

"This thing is getting out of control, Leon," I said. "I was afraid it would. Did you know my client is staying here?"

"No. I didn't. Why in the world would you take that kind of risk?"

"I just thought it would be best. I thought he'd be safer here than in Collierville with his parents or just out on his own. I thought I could protect him. I guess I was wrong."

"He's still alive," Leon said. "You think whoever did this knew he was here?"

"I have no idea. They might have just been going after his lawyer. Maybe they didn't know that was his car. It doesn't matter, though. I'm getting him out of here. I'll talk to his parents and find him a safer place."

"Might be hard," Leon said. "There's witness protection, but I've never heard of defendant protection. After last night, you best find a cave to hide him in."

"I'll do the best I can. Did you ever talk to Erlene about the girl making the rape allegations?"

"I tried, brother Dillard, I swear I did. I went to her house. She was cold to me, rude even. She wouldn't even let me in the door. Never treated me like that before. Not once."

"But you asked her about the girl?"

"Oh, yeah, I asked her all right. And as soon as I did, fire started coming out of her eyes. She said she hoped the girl took the university for every dime it had. What was strange was that she didn't mention the boys who are charged with committing the crime. She didn't say, 'I hope those boys rot in prison,' or anything like that. She just rattled on about what a bunch of lowlifes the people that run the university are and that they deserve to pay. I got the distinct impression she'd had a run-in with them before."

"I'm going to take another shot at her," I said. "She knows something. She might even be behind this whole thing."

"Why would Erlene orchestrate a false rape claim against three black players?" Leon asked. "Doesn't make a bit of sense."

"When it comes to Erlene, you just never know what's going through that devious mind of hers. No offense. I know you care about her."

"None taken," he said. "And I don't care about her all that much anymore. The shine just sort of wore off her. Besides, I keep getting reports that she's moving more and more coke out of that hole she calls a business. I'm probably going to wind up stinging her."

"Why don't you do it now?" I said. "It could give you some leverage in trying to unravel what really happened at that party."

Leon paused and sipped his coffee. He set the cup back down on the table and said, "That party ain't my case, brother Dillard."

"Maybe not, but what did or didn't happen at that party has now caused a bunch of ripple effects. One of those effects is that your good buddy Joe Dillard's house was shot up. His life, his wife's life, his client's life and his dogs' lives were all endangered, and somebody burned a damned cross in his yard. I was hoping that might piss you off enough to forget about jurisdictional squabbles."

Leon picked the cup back up, drained it, and stood. He put his cowboy hat back on his head.

"You know what, brother Dillard? You're right. When you put it that way, you're absolutely right. It pisses me off beyond words, and I'm gonna get out there right now and start doing something about it."

FRIDAY, OCTOBER 11

Kevin came walking into the kitchen around 8:00 a.m., looking haggard and worried.

"Breakfast?" I said. "I'm a good cook."

"No thanks," he said. "I don't think I can eat right now."

"You drink coffee?"

"Not much. I'd drink some orange juice if you have it."

"In the fridge," I said. "Help yourself."

After Leon left, I'd gone into the bedroom and hung a bag of sodium chloride from an IV tower and hooked it up to Caroline's PICC line. We'd decided we'd had enough of home health care nurses for the time being. I fixed her a peach and banana smoothie with an egg in it, just like I did three or four times a week. After that, I'd called Jack and talked to both him and Charlie and had told them what happened. Jack wanted to come out, but I said there wasn't anything he could do. I wanted him to go to the office. I was supposed to meet Stony at nine, and I asked Jack and Charlie to take that meeting for me and find out what she'd learned about Mike Armstrong. I also called Stony and told her I wouldn't be at the meeting and asked her if she'd share what she'd learned with Jack and Charlie. She agreed.

Kevin poured himself a glass of orange juice and sat down at the table while I leaned against the kitchen counter and ate a bowl of strawberries and blueberries.

"You have to go," I said. "I'm sorry. I thought this would be okay, but after last night, I'm not comfortable with you being here. I'm afraid whoever did this knows you're here. I'm just not sure. The whole thing might have been directed at me because I'm representing you, but the sheriff didn't say anything about Devante's or Evan's lawyer's houses being shot up or crosses being burned in their yards. I don't know if they knew that was your car they shot all to hell, but I have to assume they did. I just don't want to take unnecessary risks. They might be watching, just waiting for a chance to get a shot at you or snatch you up. We need to call your parents and we need to find a place to hide you until I can get this thrown out or get you acquitted at trial. Any idea where you might be able to go? I wouldn't be comfortable with you staying with your parents. It'd be too easy for them to find you if they're looking."

"Who's they?" Kevin said.

"Probably the Klan or some group like them."

"I can't believe this," he said. "It's beyond anything I could have ever imagined."

"It's real," I said. "Imagine the worst possible thing that could happen, which is them getting their hands on you, and figure out where you could go to keep that from happening. I have an old Army buddy named Bo Hallgren who lives in Michigan that you could go and stay with. He lives on a big farm and would do anything I asked of him. He'd do his best to protect you."

"I don't want to put someone else in danger," he said.

"Whatever you do, wherever you go, someone is going to be in danger," I said. "Especially you. Help me out here. You're a smart young man. I need you to think in terms of survival. Imagine you're being hunted by the most dangerous predator in the world. Where would you go to hide?"

"My face has been all over newspapers and magazines and television screens everywhere in the country," Kevin said. "My best friend from high school lives in Oregon now. He's getting a master's at Oregon State in Corvalis. He texted me when I was arrested. He saw my face on the CBS Evening News. I don't think there's anywhere in the country I can go and really feel safe. I might as well just stay here and ride it out. If they kill me, they kill me. If you don't want me here, though, if you don't want it on your conscience if they get to me or if you're afraid they'll hurt you or your wife, I understand. I'll go to Collierville and stay with my parents."

I shook my head and sighed.

"I guess you're right," I said. "You're probably not safe anywhere. Just stay here. Do you know how to use a gun?"

"No, sir. I've never fired a gun in my life."

"Okay. Well, I don't think they'll try anything in broad daylight. I'm sure the sheriff will have his guys keeping a close eye on the house. I'm going to go to the office and meet with someone, get some work done, and I'll be back at lunch. Do me a favor and stay in the house. Rio will let you know if anyone unwelcome comes around. If he starts barking or growling, call 911 and then call me."

"Okay," Kevin said.

I got dressed and, after sweeping shattered glass out of part of the cab of my truck, drove to the office. The back windshield of my truck had been blown out, and there were three bullet holes in the tailgate, but it was otherwise unscathed. As soon as I got a chance, I would take it to a car wash and vacuum it thoroughly. Then I'd have to take it to a body shop and get the windshield replaced and the tailgate repaired.

Stony had already arrived when I got to the office. I'd called Jack and told him I was coming, so they were waiting for me. The four of us settled into the conference room.

"This is a privileged meeting," Stony said immediately. "I want it understood from the beginning that anything that is said in this room this morning stays here, and anything I might happen to give to you did not come from me. Is that clear? I have no intentions of going to jail, and if I do, I promise you'll all go with me."

"Sounds serious," I said, knowing I was about to get some long-awaited answers to some perplexing questions.

"It is. Are we in agreement?" she said.

"Absolutely," I said.

"Are you recording this meeting in any way?"

"No," I said.

"I have your word? No audio or video recorders hidden? Nobody taking any notes?"

"Nothing."

"Mind if I sweep the office for bugs?"

"Go right ahead."

She pulled a small device out of her briefcase and began walking around the office. She was back in ten minutes.

"The place is clean," she said. "No bugs, no cameras."

"Good to know," I said.

"Okay, first. The infamous lineup. Present were Investigator Bo Riddle of the Johnson City Police Department and the alleged victim in the case, Sheila Self."

Stony pulled out a laptop and pushed it to the center of the conference room desk. Someone at the JCPD -- another investigator, I was certain – had placed a hidden camera in the ceiling above Riddle's head. Stony pushed a button on the keyboard and the video began to play. It clearly showed Riddle coaching Sheila Self. He laid out only six photos, all of them were black ETSU players in uniform, and especially with the identity of Kevin Davidson, he was clearly tapping on the photo to influence her to choose it. The audio that went along with the charade of a lineup was priceless. I absolutely could not wait to confront Riddle on a witness stand with this evidence. It would be a true Perry Mason moment.

"And when the judge asks me how I got my hands on this, what do I say?" I said to Stony.

"You're going to call Riddle as a witness, correct?"

"That's the plan."

"The first witness you need to call is Bret Marshall. He was Riddle's partner early on, only been with the department for two months. He set this up and can authenticate the video. He quit the job, and he's willing to testify."

"Are you kidding? He's willing to violate the code of silence? His career as a cop will be over."

"It's already over. He resigned as soon as he made this tape. He told me if being a cop means he has to stand by and watch things like this take place, he doesn't want to be a cop."

"Does he have another job?" I said.

"Not yet."

"Well, call him and tell him to go see Leon Bates. Leon's guys are honest. He'll hire him."

"Will do," Stony said.

"This will blow Judge Neese's head off," Jack said.

"It gets worse," Stony said.

"How much worse could it get?" Charlie said. "This is so blatant that Riddle should be fired at the very least. He should go to jail for this."

"He might," I said. "If the judge lets me use it, he'll commit perjury on the stand. Of course, it'll be up to his buddy Armstrong to prosecute him and I doubt that'll happen. But the judge could hold him in contempt and put him in jail. If she does, Gene Starring will fire him."

"I have a short recording of a telephone conversation you need to listen to."

"Okay," I said. "Who's doing the talking?"

"Mike Armstrong and a woman you know."

She pushed another key on the laptop.

Mike Armstrong: "Hello?"

Erlene Barlowe: "It's me, sugar. We need to meet."

Mike Armstrong: "Where?"

Erlene Barlowe: "Usual place."

Mike Armstrong: "Has something gone wrong?"

Erlene Barlowe: "Not yet, but you need to up the pressure. You need to make sure you nail these boys and do it in a hurry. We'll talk about it when we meet."

They hung up. That was the extent of the conversation.

"What is Erlene Barlowe doing encouraging the district attorney to 'nail these boys?'" Charlie said.

"She's doing what she does best," I said. "Pulling strings. I just have to find out exactly which ones and why."

"I can't tell you why, but I can tell you how she's manipulating him," Stony said. "I have some more recordings of Armstrong that you probably don't need to hear. I'll hang on to them in case you really need them later, but I think all you have to do is let Armstrong know about the tapes."

"Are there more recordings of Armstrong and Erlene?"

"No. He has a boyfriend, Joe. An electrician named Michael Adams. I guarantee you she knows about it. Some of the stuff I have on tape is pretty graphic. He wouldn't want it getting out. She might have the same kind of thing."

"Anything else?" I said.

"Yes, a couple of things as a matter of fact. I spoke with the officer who arrested Sheila Self. Her name is Tonya James."

"I've read her report," I said.

"One thing she didn't include in that report was that she got a judge to sign an order for a Drug Facilitated Sexual Assault panel. Armstrong has the results. Has he provided them to you in discovery?"

"No. There hasn't been any mention of it from him."

"Another thing for you to go after him on. He's withholding evidence from you that is probably exculpatory."

"What a surprise," I said.

"One last thing," Stony said. "Some of my old friends at the FBI say they've been picking up chatter from various hate groups, both white and black. They're mobilizing and they're headed this way. Both sides are looking for an armed confrontation."

"At least one side is already here," I said, "given what happened at my house."

"More are on the way."

"Great," I said. "That's just great. Do we need to start wearing bullet proof vests?"

"Might not be a bad idea. Be alert."

I stood and started toward the door.

"Where are you going?" Jack said.

"To get some equipment from my office and then to Erlene's house to see if I can put a stop to this. She won't be at work this early. Thank you, Stony. Great job. You guys finish up without me."

FRIDAY, OCTOBER 11

I pulled into Erlene's driveway a little after ten. She lived between Johnson City and Jonesborough in the Boones Creek area, not far from the chic Ridges development. Her house, which was far too large for one person, sat atop a hill on a two-acre lot surrounded by a wall of fifteen-foot-high Arborvitaes. The house itself was a Craftsman style, similar to ours. It was two story, made of stone and glass and wood with a little decorative brick thrown in. The porch was a wide wraparound and the roof was low-pitched. The grounds were perfectly manicured, and there was a large pool with a pool house and Jacuzzi in back. It was an extremely nice place.

I got out, walked up to the front door, and rang the bell. Erlene had a schnauzer named Benny, and he began barking. She opened the door after just a couple of minutes and was genuinely surprised to see me standing there.

"Why, Joe Dillard, I swan. What brings you out to my humble little abode?"

She was wearing a silk robe with a gold and black tiger print and fluffy pink slippers. Her hair was perfect, as was her make-up.

"I need to talk to you, Erlene. It's important."

"I was just having a cup of tea on the porch out back," she said. "Would you like one?"

"Sure, that'd be nice."

I followed her through the house. She had unusual tastes when it came to home décor – there were a lot of masks on the walls, a couple of Indian chief headdresses, some phallic pieces that had to have come from Africa, and several family photos. She'd told me about a couple of the photos. One was her deceased husband, Gus, who died mowing the lawn several years earlier, and another was of Gus's daughter from his first marriage, who had died in a car accident. The walls in the house were painted in bright colors – blues and reds and garish pinks. Caroline and I had been in the house a few times when Leon and Erlene were dating. Caroline said she thought a New Orleans brothel would be decorated similarly.

"Go on out, honey," she said. "I'll be right along."

I walked out onto the back porch. It had a beautiful view of the mountains that surrounded the area, and they were starting to come alive with the bright reds and oranges of fall. It was a serene setting, which made me feel a bit guilty because I was there to stir some things up.

Erlene walked out holding a cup of tea. Hers was on the table. I noticed her fingernails were painted the same tiger stripe design as her robe when she handed me the cup and saucer. The woman was nothing if not eccentric.

"What's on your mind this beautiful fall morning?" Erlene said. "And I have to say you look wonderfully handsome, just like always."

"Thank you, Erlene. I'm here, I think, to try to keep you out of jail."

Her mouth dropped open and her eyebrows raised in a perfect Erlene expression of surprise and bewilderment.

"Whatever could you possibly be talking about, sugar? I haven't done anything wrong."

"We both know that isn't true," I said. "You pimp your girls on occasion, you sell drugs out of the club, and you're not above blackmailing a customer here and there if he has enough money and you have enough goods on him. You've had people killed. I don't judge you for any of those things. Don't really care, to tell you the truth. But you're doing something with Mike Armstrong that is going to get you in deeper than you know. I might not be able to dig you out if you don't let me help you."

"How could I possibly help you? I don't even know Mike Armstrong other than what I've seen of him on television. Ugly little man. I'll say that much."

"I have a recording of you talking to him on the phone, Erlene."

She set her tea cup very slowly into the saucer, looked at me, smiled, and said, "I just don't see how that's possible, sweetie pie. I've never talked to the man."

"Yes, you have. I heard it just before I came over here. If you hear it, it'll be in court, you'll be under oath, and it won't be good for you."

"My goodness," she said. "I never thought I'd see the day when my wonderful friend Joe Dillard, who I paid half a million dollars in cash a few years ago, would threaten me."

"I earned the money," I said. "You and Angel Christian both walked on murder charges. And you were both as guilty as sin. You know it and I know it. But that's not why I'm here. I'm not here to threaten you. I'm here to ask you to help me understand what in the hell is going on with these three football players from ETSU."

"The ones who raped my Sheila?"

"They didn't rape her. I'm about to blow that case out of the water, Erlene. But it's already gotten out of hand. Do you know that somebody burned a cross in front of my house last night and shot up my garage, my truck, Caroline's car and another car? There has been so much racial tension created by this case that it's about to turn into something that will be extremely ugly and extremely violent. People could die. I'd like to know why, and I think you can tell me. If you don't, I'm afraid our relationship going forward is going to change dramatically. And when I take the tape I have and play it for Leon, I think his attitude toward you is going to change, too. You'll start having some serious problems with Leon and his deputies at your club."

"Shitdammit," Erlene said. She crossed and re-crossed her legs. "Shitdammit! Why did you have to get involved in this case? Why couldn't it have been some dimwitted lawyer like ninety percent of them are?"

"Please, just tell me what's going on and I'll do everything in my power to make sure everything turns out all right."

She stood up and started pacing back and forth in front of me, her massive bosom bouncing up and down with each step like waves rolling onto a beach. Constant motion.

"It'll ruin everything," she said. "All my plans. It'll ruin them."

"They're already ruined. You just don't know it," I said.

"No they aren't. If you could just hold off another couple of weeks, we'll have it done and you can go ahead and get your boys off the hook."

"Have what done, Erlene?"

"I can't tell you."

"You'd better tell me. I'm not messing around here, Erlene. Three young men's lives are at stake. Even if I get them released, they're still going to be in danger. You set it all in motion somehow. I want to know why."

She looked at me and spat the words like a spitting cobra: "Because those miserable fools at the university deserved it, that's why."

"Deserved what?"

"They deserved to be humiliated, they deserved to be embarrassed, and they deserve to pay through the nose."

"Why? What did they do to you?"

She composed herself, at least somewhat, and sat back down.

"I've been planning this for two years," she said. "Just waiting for the right girl, the right opportunity. Do you remember when it was announced that the hospital was renaming its new heart hospital from The Sloan-Miller Heart Hospital to just the Sloan Heart Hospital?"

"No," I said. "I don't remember that at all."

"That's because they didn't want anyone to think it was that big of a deal. They just quietly took Dr. Albert Miller's name off of the hospital. Dr. Miller was extremely wealthy – old money wealthy – and just happened to be a regular visitor to my club for a while. He taught at ETSU's medical school in the cardiology department, and he'd donated a bunch of money to the school to have his name put on the heart hospital. He was in his fifties, he was filthy rich, and he was divorced, so I guess he was lonely. He called one day and asked to speak with me. He'd found out that I owned the club and he wanted to visit, but he wanted complete privacy. He didn't want anyone knowing he was there, and he was willing to pay top dollar to make sure nobody saw him come and go. So I had one of my employees pick him up and drop him off at the back entrance to the VIP lounge at least a couple of times a week for two years. He'd come in, have his fun, and my employee would drive him home.

"During that time, there were three girls he really took a shine to. I won't tell you their names because it really doesn't matter, but what he did was, he offered to help them. He offered to help them get into college, pay their tuition, and give them enough money every month so they didn't have to work for me anymore. I was skeptical about it at first. I mean, who's that nice? Nobody, right? But he seemed sincere, and before I knew it, three of my girls were gone and so was he."

"I didn't hear anything from any of the girls for almost two months, so one day I drove by one of the girls' trailer just to see how she was doing. She was a mess. A mess. This doctor had been good to them for a little while. He never got them into school. He just kept making excuses. But he did send them money, and it was quite a bit of money for them. But then they found out the catch. There's always a catch, isn't there, sugar? I mean, nobody in this world is pure-hearted. You're the closest person I've met to having a pure heart, but you're human, aren't you sweetie? You have your moments of weakness, don't you?"

"I suppose I do, Erlene. Keep going."

She took a deep breath and said, "Well, they found out the catch was that they had to have sex with him. Whenever he wanted, wherever he wanted, all of them at the same time sometimes. And he did unspeakable things to them. I've run across some perverted men in my day, as you can imagine, but this man was at the top of the class. I don't even want to go into all the things he was making them do. It was just disgusting."

"Why didn't they come back to you, report him to the police? Maybe go to the university and tell them what he was doing?" I said.

"We did all of those things, sugar. *I* did all of those things. I would have called you but you were off in Nashville doing a big murder case down there with some record company executive. But I went to the Johnson City police. They laughed me out the door. Just refused to take the word of a few strippers over the word of a rich doctor whose name was on a heart hospital. When I went to the university, they said they didn't believe a word of it, and even if they did, it was between the doctor and the girls. The university had absolutely no responsibility whatsoever. So the next thing I did was, I went to a reporter at the Johnson City newspaper. He was nice, a real sweetie pie. He listened. He talked to the girls and he even went and talked to the doctor. It must have rattled the doctor pretty badly because he said some things he shouldn't have said and the reporter wound up writing a story about these terrible accusations my girls were making against this rich doctor. But you know what? The gutless owner of the newspaper wouldn't publish the story. He said he was afraid of being sued.

"So nothing happened to that doctor, other than they very quietly removed his name from the hospital. They placated him by naming a chair of excellence after him, though. The Dr. Albert Miller Chair of Excellence in cardiology. It's still there today and it disgusts me. *He's* still there. Can you believe that?"

I folded my arms and rocked back and forth in my chair. Erlene was as angry as I'd ever seen her, and I'd seen her angry enough to have someone killed.

"Why didn't you kill him?" I said. "Why didn't you have Ronnie pay him a visit?"

"I did have Ronnie pay him a visit," she said. "He put on a ski mask and performed a little surgery. The doctor no longer has all of his equipment."

"Ronnie castrated him?"

"No. He removed his terwilliger with a scalpel. And he didn't leave it there so the man could have it reattached. He put it in the burn barrel out back of the club."

"Terwilliger" was Erlene's pet name for a man's penis. She'd removed one herself from a preacher who had raped one of her girls not long before I first met her.

"No problems with the police?" I said.

"They came around, but Ronnie's a pro. He didn't leave anything behind for them to make any connections to us."

"And that wasn't enough for you?" I said.

"Not near enough, sugar. Not as far as I was concerned. But I had to wait for the right time, and it had to be the right girl. I thought Sheila Self was the right girl, but she turned out to be … how should I put this? Less reliable than I thought she'd be. Poor thing. She's been through so much I should have known better, but she was a student at the university, and that was the key to this whole thing."

"How? What difference did it make that she was a student?"

"I'm not the brightest bulb, but I'm not the dullest, either," Erlene said. "I figured the best way to get back at the university was by doing two things. Embarrassing them in front of God and everybody and suing the pants off of them, no pun intended. I started researching suing universities and I learned about this Title IX. Do you know what Title IX is, sweetie?"

"I do. It protects women from discrimination on college campuses. It also protects them from sexual assault, or at least it's supposed to."

"That's right, so when a call came into the escort service looking for a girl to dance at a party for football players on campus, I immediately thought of Sheila and I thought we could pull this off."

"What, exactly, did you tell her to do?"

"I told her to go to the party, to be friendly, and to go into the bathroom and take just a little GHB. GHB loosens a person up, you know what I mean, sweetie? It lowers people's inhibitions. Then I told her to come out, start her show, and to make sure she touched several of them. I told her to scratch a few of them lightly and get some DNA under her fingernails. I told her to give free lap dances if she had to, to run her fingers through their hair. And then I told her to leave, wait an hour, and call the police and tell them she'd been raped. But she drank beer and took ecstasy and had sex with her worthless boyfriend before she went to the party, and then she took too much GHB. Apparently, she was barely able to do anything at all. She wound up leaving, but she doesn't remember any of it. She wound up getting picked up by a cop later and told the cop she'd been raped."

"Gang raped?" I said.

"I didn't say anything about gang raped, and I didn't say anything about black players. She and the investigator cooked up every bit of that later. I had no way of knowing he'd do something so stupid and hateful, but in a way, it's helped our case because the university is about to pay out a bunch of money. They're terrified those boys might get convicted and if they wait, they may have to pay a bunch more."

"Who's going to get this money, Erlene?"

"The lawyer I hired out of Nashville will get forty percent, the greedy pig. Sheila will get seventy percent of what's left, and then I plan to take a cut."

"So Sheila made up the story about being gang raped, and the cop turned it into a black on white thing?"

"Sheila says he's a full-blown racist, but she doesn't have any love for black men either. She was assaulted by two black boys in high school and when she retaliated, she was the one who wound up getting sent off to juvy."

"Yeah, I heard that story," I said. "She took a butcher knife to a fellow student. That'll get you sent off every time."

"They were harassing her, feeling her up," Erlene said. "Don't take their side."

"I'm not. So the big question for me is, what is Mike Armstrong's angle in all this? How have you gotten him to continue with this prosecution? He doesn't have diddly as far as evidence goes."

"Everybody has their skeletons," Erlene said. "I'm good at finding them. I put a private investigator on him as soon as he was appointed to the district attorney's office. Just in case. You never know when some good, old-fashioned dirt might come in handy. I do the same thing with judges and assistant DAs, the chief of police, and even the sheriff. Anybody that might be a potential threat to me and my being able to make a living, I have a file on them. I started doing DAs after that terrible man Deacon Baker charged my Angel with murder and then turned around and charged me when you got Angel off."

"You said the sheriff. Do you have a file on Leon?"

"Of course. I have some wonderful movies of him and me together doing some things I'm sure he'd rather not become public knowledge."

"You might be the most devious person I've ever met," I said.

She winked and smiled at me. "I'll take that as a compliment, sugar."

"So you're blackmailing Armstrong?"

"That sounds a bit harsh, sweetie, but yes, I suppose I am. I'm also paying him. If this goes as planned – which means if you don't ruin it – I'm going to pay him two hundred thousand dollars."

"What kind of dirt do you have on him?"

"Something he doesn't want anyone to know. It's like I said, everyone has secrets. I'll bet even you have a few, although I confess I don't know what they are and wouldn't for the life of me ever use them against you even if I did."

"What doesn't he want anyone to know, Erlene?"

"Do you know what the seven deadly sins are, baby doll?"

I thought for a moment. Seven deadly sins. Originated with the Catholics, I thought.

"I'm not sure," I said. "Pride, maybe? Envy? Gluttony? I don't remember all of them off-hand."

"You got three right. They're pride, greed, lust, envy, gluttony, wrath and sloth. Everybody's guilty at one time or another. That's why we shouldn't be so quick to judge each other, but we are. People are quick to judge, and the juicier the sin, the harsher the judgment."

"Armstrong," I said.

'Lust. He's having an affair. With a man. He's very sneaky about it, but my investigator caught him with his pants down, so to speak. I have photos, videos, recordings, everything I need to destroy him if he doesn't do what I want."

"And remind me what it is exactly that you want?"

"For him to keep this prosecution going long enough for me to get a big check out of the university. I want to take a bite out of them so big they'll feel it for a long time to come, and I'm right on the verge of getting it done. Please don't ruin it for me. I've waited and planned for so long. Just give me a couple more weeks."

"I'm going to have to think this over," I said as I stood to leave.

"We've been friends for a long time, sugar," Erlene said. "Please don't let me down."

I went out to my bullet-riddled truck and left. I felt a pang of guilt as I drove away.

I had a small camera in my tie clasp along with a microphone.

I'd taped every bit of the conversation.

PART THREE

MONDAY, OCTOBER 14

C harlie, Jack and I had gathered the forensic toxicology report from Dr. Kershaw that showed how much
GHB was in Sheila Self's system the night they drew
blood from her at the hospital, the results from the DNA
testing done by the TBI lab in Knoxville, the audio/video
recording of Investigator Riddle and Sheila Self doing the
bogus lineup, the audio recording of the phone conversation between Erlene and Armstrong, the video/audio
I had of Erlene, and had spent the weekend drafting a
motion to dismiss the indictments against the players for
violations of the defendants' fourteenth amendment right
to due process under the law. The motion also alleged
bad faith on the part of the prosecution. I shared it with
Patrick Lonon, the public defender who was representing Devante Wright, and with Jim Beaumont, who was
representing Evan Belle, and asked whether they wanted
to sign on. Both of them did.

My biggest problem was that there was no way I'd get
the conversation between Mike Armstrong and Erlene
Barlowe into court. It was illegal in Tennessee to record
a telephone conversation without the consent of at least
one party. I could record someone calling me because I

consented to the recording, but I couldn't intercept and record a conversation between two individuals without the consent of at least one of them or without a court order or a warrant. I had neither of those things.

The question of what I would do with the knowledge of Mike Armstrong's affair was delicate. I didn't want to out him in public. It was beneath me, but he had to know that I knew why he was continuing this farce of a case. I figured we'd handle that matter in the judge's chambers if I could get the judge to agree.

What I was most looking forward to was getting Bo Riddle on the witness stand. I knew once I filed the motion it would become a part of the public record and the media would jump all over it. The motion hearing would be packed and probably be covered by at least some national media outlets. It would be a big stage, but I'd been on some pretty big stages before with a lot at stake. I was ready. Charlie had run the motion over to the courthouse early on Monday (Washington County hadn't yet moved into the digital age which would have allowed us to file everything electronically) and I'd called the judge. The motion hearing was set for Thursday.

On Monday morning about ten-thirty, I was sitting at my desk going back over everything when Beverly Snyder's voice came over the intercom on my desk.

"There's a man here who is asking to see you, Mr. Dillard," she said. "Actually, he's demanding to see you. He doesn't have an appointment."

"Does he have a name?"

"He won't give me his name. I think you should come out here."

I recognized a strain in Beverly's voice. She was frightened.

"Be right out," I said.

Our renovation of the office had included some security measures. One of those measures was that Jack, Charlie and I all had weapons in our offices. I had a Sig Sauer nine-millimeter pistol taped under my desk that I could get to very easily. It was pointed at the chair that sat in front of my desk and if I had to, I could fire it through the desk without the person who was sitting there ever knowing what was coming. I didn't look at it as radical. I looked at it as practical. A few years earlier, a deranged man who had become obsessed with Charlie had come into the office and tried to kill her. He shot Jack in the process. Besides that, we dealt with some pretty dangerous folks, and lawyers had been killed in their offices by victims of crimes, by family members of victims of crimes, and by their own clients. I didn't intend to become just another dead lawyer, murdered by some nut in my office. Jack also had a nine-millimeter pistol in his office and Charlie had a sawed-off shotgun loaded with twelve-gauge slugs that would take someone's head off. She knew how to use, it, too. Everyone had panic buttons on the floor beneath our desks that we could push with our feet. If I pushed the button in my office, a red light began flashing in everyone else's office. Panic button meant gun or knife or some other deadly weapon had been displayed. Our strategy was to shoot first if we had to. Our goal was to survive. We'd let the cops sort things out later.

The pistol beneath my desk was a semi-automatic. There was a round in the chamber. I reached down, cocked the hammer, and flipped the safety off before I went into the lobby. Once I got there, I saw a large black man towering over Beverly, who was sitting behind her desk.

"Can I help you?" I said.

He turned and looked at me with disdain. He was taller than me, maybe six-feet-four-inches, and muscular. He looked to be in his early, maybe mid-thirties and was wearing jeans and a black leather jacket over a black T-shirt. I looked down and noticed he was wearing combat boots.

"I want to talk to you," he said.

"C'mon back," I said, hoping to get him away from Beverly as quickly as possible. I turned my back to him and walked into my office. He followed and closed the door behind him.

I reached out my hand and said, "I'm Joe Dillard. How can I help you?"

He looked at my hand and snorted. I withdrew the hand and said, "Would you like to sit?"

I motioned to the chair that was right in front of my desk, the one the pistol was aimed at. I was growing more concerned by the second. This guy was obviously hostile, and he had tattoos running all the way up his neck. I recognized them immediately as prison tats. One of them depicted an open, bleeding wound across his throat, as though it had been cut. I also noticed the EWMN tattoo on his fingers, which I knew meant "evil, wicked, mean and nasty." He had four gold front teeth.

He sat down in front of me, glaring, trying to intimidate me. His eyes were dark and intense, his hairline slightly receding.

"Listen," I said. "You're here in my office. You're all tatted up and you're trying to intimidate me, but you might as well know on the front end it isn't working. I'm not afraid of you."

"You should be," he said.

"What do you want?"

"I want to know what a cracker like you is doing representing my oppressed brother. I want to know what you're doing to get him out of this trumped up bullshit charge."

"First off, if you call me cracker again I'm going to come across this desk and knock those gold teeth out of your mouth. We clear on that? Secondly, I was hired to represent him by his parents. There aren't exactly a bunch of black lawyers around here in case you haven't noticed. Now I don't know who you are or who you think you are, but I don't talk about my clients with strangers. You want to know what I'm doing? Read the paper, watch the news, come to court."

"I represent an organization," he said. "Let's just say we're tired of seeing the black man being beaten down by the white man and we're ready to do something about it."

"Good for you. I agree with you that blacks have been mistreated for centuries, that things haven't changed nearly as much as they should have, and that something needs to be done about it. So we have some common ground. I also had the displeasure of having a cross burned in my yard not long ago and my house shot to hell. The people who belong to the organization that burned the cross are very similar to you. They're filled with hate. I can tell by looking at you. You don't want justice. You just want blood."

"You and me ain't got no common ground," he said, "But you're right about one thing. We're ready for war."

"Are you talking about a shooting war? Then you're right, we don't have any common ground. You start shooting and everybody will lose. You start shooting and you're just plain stupid. And you know what? You can't fix stupid, mister."

He shook his head and glared at me. I was baiting him, but I wanted him to either make his move or get the hell out of my office.

"Did you just call me stupid?" he said, the tension growing thicker by the second.

"I think maybe I did. I was pretty clear about it, actually. Now, if there's nothing productive that is going to come of this, and I don't see that there is, you can feel free to get up and walk out the door any time."

He reached inside his jacket and pulled out a revolver. It was a damned hand cannon. A Dirty Harry special, .44 Magnum. He pointed it at my face. It was as though I was looking directly down the barrel of a howitzer.

"You best start showing me some respect, boy, or you ain't gonna walk out of this room alive. Now I need for you to tell me exactly what you're doing for my brothers. I need to hear from you that they're going to walk away from these charges. You're supposed to be the man around here. You've got the reputation. I hear you have influence. Why haven't you been able to make this go away? Or are you a part of the white man's conspiracy to further smear the reputations of young black men? They're all drug dealers and gang bangers and murderers and rapists, right?"

As soon as I saw the gun, I pushed the panic button. Just as he finished his little speech, Jack walked through the door, pistol up, and moved a few steps to the right. Charlie followed with the shotgun and moved to the left. We had him triangulated. He turned around to look at them and I pulled the Sig from under the desk and stood. I pointed it at his head.

"You said you wanted a shooting war," I said. "Looks like you found one."

He looked over both shoulders and back at me.

"You don't have the nerve," he said.

"I've killed Cubans and Colombians," I said. "Your life won't be the first I've taken. Jack over there is a crack shot with that pistol and he'd kill you in a heartbeat to save his dad. If you notice, his hand isn't shaking. And Miss Charleston there? She's been up against mobsters from Philadelphia. They're dead. She's standing over there pointing a twelve-gauge at the back of your head. You picked the wrong lawyers to terrorize. Now I think the best thing for you to do right now is to lower that pistol and lay it on the floor at your feet. I could have you arrested, but you'd be out on bail in a few hours, so I'm not going to bother. I could even kill you since you pulled that gun and pointed it at me. But I'm going to let you walk out of here alive. Your gun stays."

He was staring at me, trying to figure out whether I'd really shoot him. Something, either in my eyes or in my voice, convinced him that I would. He put the gun on the floor.

"Stand up," I said.

He stood.

"Turn around and walk toward the door. We're going to accompany you to your vehicle to make sure you don't have friends waiting outside."

He started walking toward the door with the three of us behind him. No one was talking. The only sounds were feet slowly moving across the floor and measured breathing. It was one of the tensest moments of my life, and I'd been through some pretty tense times. For some reason, my fingers were tingling.

When he got to the door leading outside, he bolted. He ran right towards Sarah's diner and then ducked to the right at the end of the building. Jack started after him, but I grabbed him by the arm.

"Let him go," I said.

"This isn't good, Dad," Jack said. "You should have called the police and had him arrested."

"And put an even bigger target on my chest? No, thanks. I don't know what it is with these people. Black militants, white supremacists. Why does everybody want to kill the lawyer? Why do they want to kill each other?"

"It's an inherent flaw of the male gender," Charlie said. "They want power and control and are willing to use violence to obtain what they want. History is full of examples. Men killing men. Men killing women and children. Men devising more efficient means of killing. And for what? Power and control."

"Thank you, Charlie, for making me feel better about being a man," I said.

"I wasn't talking about you specifically," she said. "But history has proven men to be bloodthirsty, and we're in a volatile situation, the kind of situation that attracts bloodthirsty men. We haven't seen the last of him."

"Well, at least he knows there are consequences if he tries to come in here and intimidate us again," Jack said.

"He won't," I said. "He, along with some of his friends, will bushwhack us instead."

TUESDAY, OCTOBER 15

A t a convenience store in Hampton, Tennessee, the two men looked at each other from twenty feet apart. There was vague recognition on the part of Greg Murray. The man who was pumping gas into a large diesel pick-up looked familiar, but he hadn't seen him in a long, long time. Who was he? He was a mountain of a man, broad shouldered with a long brown beard, wearing the clothing of a logger. The man kept glancing over at him. Murray thought the recognition must be mutual, but the connection just hadn't quite been made.

Murray finished pumping gas into his own pick-up and was turning to get into the cab when he noticed the large man walking toward him.

"I know you," the man said.

"I know you, too. I just can't place you."

"Mind if I ask your name?"

"Greg Murray."

"Well, I'll be damned." The big man stuck out his hand.

"Garrett Brown, Greg. Long time no see, my friend."

"Yeah, it's been awhile. How have you been, Garrett?"

Garrett Brown had been a legendary athlete at Cloudland High School in Roan Mountain. He was the biggest, strongest, fastest boy at the school, and he excelled at everything he tried, except for in the classroom. Murray had played on the football and basketball teams, too, but he wasn't near the player Brown had been. They'd been friends throughout high school, close friends, in fact. They rode the mountain back roads together, drank beer and moonshine, smoked weed, chased girls, and listened to everything from Hank Williams to Lynard Skynard to Joe Cocker.

After high school, though, Murray was involved in a serious car accident that fractured his sternum, several ribs and broke his right humerus and left femur. He was in the hospital for weeks, and when he was released, he was addicted to opiates. At the time, there was no program for weaning patients who had been using large amounts of opiates while in the hospital off of the drugs, so Murray was left to either quit cold turkey and go through the terrible withdrawal symptoms or keep on trying to get his hands on the drugs any way he could. That meant going to the street dealers, and they were expensive. He'd started breaking into houses, he'd stolen from his parents and grandparents. Eventually, he found himself alone, ostracized from his family, and that's when he decided to rob a bank. He was caught and sent to the federal penitentiary.

"I was sorry to hear about what happened to you," Brown said. "How long have you been out?"

"Just a few months."

"Got a job?"

"Yeah. I'm working at a place down in Jonesborough. My mother helped me get this truck because I've been clean for several years. Just trying to put my life back together."

"How was it?" Brown said. "Prison, I mean."

Murray shrugged his shoulders. He didn't know what Brown wanted to hear.

"It was prison," he said. "I spent five years in a medium security federal pen in Beckley, West Virginia, and then they moved me to a camp. Medium was a bitch."

"A lot of niggers in there?" Brown said.

Murray was surprised by Brown's casual use of one of the most volatile words in the English language.

"Yeah, there were a lot of black guys, but if you kept your head up and stayed smart, you could avoid trouble with them. Everything in prison is organized by race. They call them cars. If I'm white and I don't want to run with a gang, then I'm automatically sorted into the Independent White Boy car. Black guys ride in their own cars, whether they're gang banging or not. It's not a good idea to mix with guys from another race in prison."

"Why do you call them black guys?" Brown said. "They're niggers, pure and simple."

"Using that word was the quickest way I knew of to get yourself shanked or killed on the inside. Even if you didn't say it to a black guy. There are no secrets in prison. The white supremacists say it all the time, but they're close to each other all the time and they protect each other. If I was talking to a white guy who wasn't an Aryan or a member of one of the other white supremacist gangs and I used that word, I'd either get blackmailed, shanked, raped or killed eventually. That's just the way it works. I just call them black guys."

"You'll get used to the change," Brown said.

"You still up on Buck Mountain?" Murray said.

"Sure am. Won't ever leave. What about you?"

"I've got a place in Washington County close to where I'm working. I come up here to see momma and daddy pretty regular. At least there aren't any black families living up there on Buck. You shouldn't have any trouble with them."

"Well, you'd be wrong about that, my friend," Brown said. "I'm real concerned about the way things are going in this country, and me and some of my buddies have decided to do something about it. Say, you wouldn't be interested in coming to a meeting, would you? We could use a man with your experience. You might be able to provide some insight."

"Insight into what?"

"Into how these niggers think. You had to be around them enough in prison to know how they think. I don't understand them. I'm sure you've heard about what's going on with those three football players raping that white girl at ETSU. We plan to do something about it. Well, just between me and you and that gas pump over there, we already did a little something about it."

Sarah had told Murray about the cross being burned in her brother's yard and the shots being fired. He had a strong suspicion that he was looking at the man – or at least one of the men – responsible.

"What'd you do?" Murray said.

"Just raised some hell. Sent a message."

"Good for you," Murray said. "I've always said a man has to act on what he believes in, not just talk about it."

"So what about that meeting? My brother and a couple of my cousins and some other boys I recruited will be there. It's a planning session. We're going to make a statement that'll be heard all over this country. The white man is going to push back against all this liberal bullshit that's been shoved down our throats."

Murray wanted nothing to do with Brown or any meeting, but he saw a chance to perhaps redeem himself for some of the things he'd done in the past and maybe learn more about what happened at Sarah's brother's house. He nodded.

"Sure, Garrett, I'll come to the meeting. I appreciate you asking me. And you're right. Maybe I *can* help."

"Damn, brother, that's good to hear," Brown said. "You know the old white Pentecostal church about a mile from my folks' place on Buck Mountain Road?"

"Yeah, I remember it."

"It ain't a church no more, but it works just fine for a meeting place. We'll be there at eight tomorrow night. Come on by and we'll fill you in on what's going to happen."

"I'll see you there," Murray said.

"Good to see you, brother," Brown said. "And welcome home. You came back at a perfect time."

WEDNESDAY, OCTOBER 16

arah called me at ten o'clock at night and asked if she could come over. I asked whether anything was wrong and she said her friend Greg Murray needed to talk to me and yes, something might be wrong. I told her to come on.

They arrived about forty minutes later. Caroline was already asleep – she was spending about twenty hours a day in bed since the radiation on her knee – and Kevin was in Jack's room. I didn't know what the conversation was going to be about, but I didn't want Kevin to listen, so when they arrived we went out on the deck. It was chilly – around forty-five degrees – but not too uncomfortable. Rio took the opportunity to disappear into the darkness and go on patrol.

This was my first time I'd seen Murray up close. He was a decent enough looking guy, a few years younger than Sarah and me. He was just under six feet tall, blonde hair that he wore medium length, pale blue eyes and a cleft chin. He was wearing jeans and work boots and a black and blue flannel shirt beneath a gray down jacket. He wasn't wearing any jewelry at all and I didn't notice any tattoos.

Sarah introduced us and we sat down.

"Can I get anybody anything?" I said. "I can make some coffee or hot tea. I have a few beers in the fridge."

"No, thanks," Murray said. Sarah also politely refused.

"I saw you the day I came down to see Sarah," I said to Murray. "I should have introduced myself."

"I was a little rude," Murray said. "I've heard a lot about you. To be honest, I was a little scared of you."

"Well, as you can see, there's nothing to be afraid of. I don't breathe fire or anything," I said.

"Do you know about my past?" he said.

I nodded. "I had the sheriff checking you out less than five minutes after I saw you that day."

"I'm clean now," he said. "I drink a beer now and then, but that's it. You don't have to worry about me being around Grace or your sister."

"I'm not," I said. "My sister has had her own struggles. She can take care of herself. And if she was the least bit concerned about you being around Grace, well… I don't even have to say any more about that. So my curiosity is piqued. What's important at this time of night?"

"I need your word you won't tell anyone I talked to you," he said.

"Okay. You have my word."

"Seriously. I could wind up dead."

"Sounds ominous. You have my word."

"I was born and raised on Buck Mountain up in Carter County," Murray said. "Ever heard of it?"

I nodded. "I've represented a few folks from up there. I've sampled a little Buck Mountain special reserve moonshine. It nearly blew the top of my head off."

Murray chuckled. "Yeah, my granddaddy used to have a still. He made some wicked stuff. So anyway, my folks are both still alive and still live up there so I go visit them on occasion. Yesterday was one of those occasions. I stopped at a convenience store in Hampton to get gas on my way back and ran into an old high school buddy of mine, a man by the name of Garrett Brown. Ring a bell?"

"Can't say that it does."

"Garrett was a big shot in high school and we were close. We ran around a lot together, got in some mischief, chased girls. You know how high school boys do. Well, I ran into him at the convenience store and we got to talking. He knew I'd been in the pen for a long time, so I guess he thought I would naturally be a candidate for what he had in mind, but I'm not. I don't want to have anything to do with what he has in mind."

"What's he have in mind?" I said. "Since you're here, I assume it has something to do with me?"

"He's a member of the Klan. He invited me to a meeting tonight. I'd just come from there when I went to Sarah's and she called you. You apparently have some big hearing scheduled tomorrow at the courthouse in Jonesborough, right?"

I nodded. "I'm hoping to put an end to the prosecution of the three young black men that were charged with raping the white woman at the football party back in August."

"They're planning an attack," he said. "They had a bulletin board up with a bunch of pictures that he said are going to be the targets. All three of the boys' pictures were up there, plus you and your son and the woman who practices law at your office."

"You mean Charlie Story?"

"Yes. Charleston Story was what he called her. They also plan to shoot those other lawyers and any black person they can shoot."

"How are they planning to do it?" I said. "Are they going to come in the building and shoot it out with the bailiffs?"

"No. They're going to have scouts in the courtroom and in the parking lot. They'll be waiting at different locations nearby. Once they get word the hearing is over and people are coming out, they're going to come tearing in the lot in pick-up trucks and start blasting away. They want to try to kill as many as they can in a minute and then get out."

"How many will there be?"

"I'm not sure," Murray said, "but Garrett mentioned other 'brothers' from different counties around here that will be involved. I'm guessing they'll have at least twenty shooters."

"And you're supposed to be one of them?"

"I told him I would, but I'm not going anywhere near that place. I don't have any desire to be involved in any kind of violence, and I'm not a racist."

"Did they give you any kind of instructions on where to meet up with anyone?"

"Yeah, there's a power station near the end of Bugaboo Springs Road. It's six or seven minutes from the courthouse, they said."

"I know where it is."

"I'm supposed to meet them there. They told me to bring a rifle, but I'm a convicted felon. I don't have a rifle. So they told me they'd have one there for me."

"Do you know the sheriff here? His name is Leon Bates."

"Heard of him. Never met him."

"He and I are friends. He's a good guy, honest as they come. He's also in charge of the security at the courthouse. Would you be willing to share with him what you just told me?"

Murray nodded. "I don't see why not."

"Good. Let me get him on the phone and get him over here. He'll want to hear this in person, and I'm sure he'll have a lot of questions."

"Oh, I almost forgot," Murray said. "Garrett and his buddies burned the cross and shot up your house. They bragged about it to me. The worst thing was they had a cop with them when they did it. Some investigator from Johnson City. He was at the meeting."

"You catch his name?" I said.

"Yeah. It was Riddle. Bo Riddle."

THURSDAY, OCTOBER 17

L eon came over the night before and spoke with Greg
Murray for an hour-and-a-half. I knew he was deeply
concerned, as was I. I told him about the black man
who paid us a visit at the office, and he said he'd been
contacted by the FBI. Apparently, the New Black Panther
Party had mobilized some of its members and a confrontation – more likely a firefight – was very likely to occur
no matter what the outcome of the hearing. Erlene's grand
plan to extort money out of the university had gone terribly wrong. Her platform had been hijacked by extremists, and I'd never known of anything good to come of
extremism in any form.

I arrived at the courthouse with Jack and Charlie
at 8:30 a.m. The security was like nothing I'd ever
seen in Jonesborough. There were armed Washington
County deputies in SWAT gear everywhere, there were
Tennessee Highway Patrolmen, there were Johnson City
and Jonesborough policemen in uniform. I'd talked to
Jack and Charlie about the possibility of violence after
the hearing and told them both to stay inside the building until we were certain it was safe to come out. We
were ready to blow Mike Armstrong's case, and possibly

his career, out of the water. We were ready to expose Sheila Self as a liar, Bo Riddle as a racist, and Erlene Barlowe as a blackmailer, extortionist, and manipulator. If all went according to plan (and things rarely did) Kevin Davidson and his teammates would be free by the afternoon. I just hoped they would still be alive.

I saw Leon standing near the front entrance to the courtroom. He, too, was dressed like a soldier about to go into combat. I walked up to him and said, "What's the play, Leon? Are you going to try to find them or wait for them to come?"

"We only have the one location that Murray gave me last night," Leon said. "We're watching it and we'll neutralize them as soon as they gather. We have everybody on deck. Patrol cars are searching. We have people in the air. We're going to do all we can to prevent bloodshed, but I'll be honest with you, brother Dillard. I have a bad feeling in the pit of my gut."

"Stay safe, my friend," I said to him and I patted him on the shoulder. "I'll see you later on."

Judge Neese walked through the door at 9:00 a.m. sharp. She sat down at the bench after the bailiff had called the court to order and looked out over the packed courtroom.

"I just want everyone here to know I won't tolerate any outbursts of any kind," she said. "None. I'll clear the courtroom."

She then turned her gaze to me. It was not sympathetic or friendly.

"Mr. Dillard, the motion you filed is, by far, the most accusatory, inflammatory, and perhaps dangerous motion that has ever been filed in my court. I'm going to give you one chance to withdraw the motion. If you fail to do so and then fail to prove the very serious allegations you've made, you will be leaving this courtroom in handcuffs. Do you understand?"

I stood and said, "I understand, your Honor. I do not wish to withdraw the motion. All I ask is that you give me a fair hearing, and I have no reason to believe you won't."

"I don't expect the kind of rhetoric and theatrics you displayed the last time you appeared before me," she said.

"I'll do my best to hold off on the rhetoric, but there are going to be some theatrics. This is a highly-charged, emotional case, as you well know. There are racial overtones that are going to be exposed here today. I hope you'll allow me to prove the allegations I've made."

"Provided you present your proof within the boundaries of the law, you'll get your chance."

"Thank you, your Honor. That's all I can ask."

"All right," the judge said. "For the record, I have before me a lengthy motion filed by Mr. Dillard and his associates and joined by counsel for the other two defendants in this case. At its core, it alleges a bad faith prosecution on the part of the district attorney general that has deprived the defendants in this case of their rights to due process under the Fourteenth Amendment to the United States Constitution and Article One, Section Nine of the Tennessee Constitution. We have several witnesses that Mr. Dillard has subpoenaed, including the alleged victim.

Mr. Armstrong did not try to quash the subpoena, so I can only conclude that he has no problem with his alleged victim being subjected to examination by Mr. Dillard prior to trial."

I looked over at Armstrong, wondering whether he had talked with Erlene. I was sure he had, because he looked like he'd just eaten a pile of horse manure and was ready to throw up. I was thinking he knew he was about to be run over by a train, there was no way he could stop it, and he just wanted to get on with it. He hadn't filed any sort of written response to the motion, hadn't asked to keep anything out or exclude any witnesses. I wondered whether he'd even bothered to read it.

"Call your first witness, Mr. Dillard," the judge said.

"We call Laurie Ingram," I said.

A pretty young woman with curly brown hair and dark eyes, dressed in a thigh-length blue dress, walked into the courtroom and sat down in the witness chair. She raised her hand and was sworn in by the judge.

"Objection," Mike Armstrong said. "We object to the relevance of this witness's testimony."

"Do you even know what the testimony is going to be?" the judge said.

"Mr. Dillard hasn't bothered to inform me," Armstrong said.

"Your honor, this young lady took a video that we intend to play for the court. I tried to play it for Mr. Armstrong, but he refused to watch. I sent him a copy last week. He obviously hasn't bothered to look at it. The video depicts what happened at the party where this alleged rape occurred, the witness can authenticate it, and it's relevant to the issues in the motion we filed."

"Objection overruled," the judge said. "Go ahead, Mr. Dillard."

"Would you state your name, please?" I said.

"Laurie Ingram."

"Miss Ingram, back on the night of Saturday, August twenty-fourth and early morning of Sunday, August twenty-fifth, did you attend a party held by the majority of the members of East Tennessee State University's football team?"

"I did."

"How many people were there?"

"I'm not sure, maybe sixty or seventy."

"And why were you there?"

"I was dating one of the players. He asked me to come along. He said a stripper was coming and it might be fun. I'd never seen a stripper, so I went."

"What time did you arrive at the party, Miss Ingram?"

"Around eleven-thirty, I think. Give or take a few minutes."

"Was the dancer already there when you arrived?"

"No. She didn't show up until midnight. She got out of a cab and when I saw what she was wearing, I told myself, 'I have to video this.' So I pointed my phone at her and started the video."

"You started as soon as she got there?"

"As soon as she stepped out of the cab."

"Your Honor," I said, "we'd like to play the digital recording at this time."

"Go ahead," the judge said.

Jack had the recording on his laptop, which he had blue-toothed to the large monitor on the wall of the courtroom to my right. Everyone looked up as the video began. It showed the time and the date. It showed Sheila Self stepping up onto the curb as her cab pulled away. She was dressed in skin-tight, red spandex, fishnet stockings, and stiletto heels. She was carrying a clutch purse in one hand and a boom box in the other. She walked up the short sidewalk as the video camera followed her, and went through the front door into a room full of young men who were whooping and hollering. She seemed lucid enough, friendly and smiling. She waved at several of the players. Laurie Ingram must have been intrigued, because she stayed within five feet of Sheila.

Sheila didn't touch any of the players, and none of them attempted to touch her. You could hear her say very plainly, "Where can I freshen up just a bit, handsome?" to one of the players. She was directed to a room about ten feet away. She went into the room and closed the door. I asked Jack to stop the tape.

"Miss Ingram," I said. "Do you happen to know what room the young lady just went into?"

"It's a bathroom," she said. "There are two bathrooms in the house. That was one of them."

"How long was she in there?"

"Objection," Armstrong said. "Calls for speculation."

"She stopped the tape when the dancer went into the bathroom," I said. "But she started it again as soon as she came out. If we can just resume the tape it'll tell us exactly how long she was in the room. It's time-stamped."

Sheila came out seven minutes and forty-seven seconds later. When she did, she was like a different person. Her eyes were droopy, she was moving slowly, and when she tried to speak, it was unintelligible. It took her a full five minutes to get her boom box positioned, set up and turned on. Once the music started, she was totally incapable of dancing and nearly incapable of staying upright. She stumbled around the room for a couple of minutes before falling flat on her face. Two people reached out to help her, but she cursed them and told them not to touch her. After a few minutes, a few of the players started to boo. The chorus grew louder, and Sheila threw up her middle finger. She mumbled a racial slur and turned to walk out the door. Another young woman who was at the party grabbed her boom box and clutch purse and carried them outside. She handed them to Sheila while people behind them yelled about her returning their money and others hooted and laughed.

Sheila pulled a wad of cash out of her clutch purse and threw it at the groups of players outside. While they gathered up bills, she staggered up the street and was gone less than twenty minutes after she arrived. The tape showed her disappearing over a small rise at 12:18 a.m.

"Miss Ingram, after this young lady's initial visit to the bathroom, did she return to that room?"

"No, sir. She left."

"You didn't witness anyone dragging her into the bathroom?"

"No, sir."

"You didn't hear any sounds of struggle? You didn't hear her crying out for help?"

"No, sir. She couldn't even talk."

"She didn't come out of the bathroom later and claim she'd been raped?"

"No, sir. What you just saw on the tape is exactly what happened."

"Thank you, Miss Ingram. Please answer Mr. Armstrong's questions."

Armstrong stood, cleared his throat, and straightened his tie.

"How much did Mr. Dillard pay you for that recording?" he said.

I started to object, but I knew the answer so I kept my mouth shut.

"He didn't pay me anything. The young woman over there, Miss Story, she was the one who found me and asked if I'd taped anything at the party. I showed it to her and she asked if they could make a copy."

"Has the tape we've just seen been altered in any way from the copy you gave Miss Story?"

"No, sir. It's exactly the same."

"Are you positive?"

"Objection," I said. "Argumentative. Asked and answered."

"Sustained. Move on, Mr. Armstrong."

"How long after you recorded this did you leave the party?" Armstrong said.

"About five minutes. It got pretty rowdy in the front yard for a few minutes and I was afraid the police would come. So my boyfriend and I left."

"So you have no way of knowing whether Miss Self, the dancer, returned later on, do you?"

"Objection," I said. "There's no foundation for the question. Their entire narrative has been that she was raped at the party and now he's trying to say she may have returned and been raped later? She was in a police car an hour later and then went to the hospital. That's all documented. I object."

"Sustained," the judge said.

"That's all I have," Armstrong said, and he sat down.

"Next witness, Mr. Dillard," Judge Neese said.

"We call Bret Marshall," I said.

Marshall, who was Bo Riddle's partner at the Johnson City Police Department for a very short time, walked into court wearing a brown suit over a white button-down shirt. He was just a kid, maybe twenty-five, with light brown hair cut very short, clean shaven, and green eyes.

"State your name, please," I said.

"Bret David Marshall."

"Mr. Marshall, you were an investigator with the Johnson City Police Department when my client was initially interviewed there, weren't you?"

"I was."

"But you don't work there anymore, do you?"

"No, I resigned about a month after your client was interviewed."

"And why did you resign?"

"Because I knew I was going to break what is called the Blue Wall of Silence, and once I did that, I knew I'd be ostracized within the department. I'd eventually be forced out, and I wouldn't be able to find work at another police agency."

"Would you explain the Blue Wall of Silence you just mentioned?"

"It's an unwritten code among police officers – an understanding – that you do not rat out another officer even if he's done something illegal."

"And do you plan to testify that you witnessed illegal behavior on the part of another officer?"

"I do."

"Which officer is that, Mr. Marshall?"

"Investigator Bo Riddle."

"And what did Investigator Riddle do that was illegal?"

"He assaulted your client, for starters, by kneeing him in the testicles, and then he brought the alleged victim in and conducted a totally ridiculous photo lineup with her. He coached her into picking the three players who have been charged."

"Did you witness this lineup?"

"In a manner of speaking. I set up a pinhole camera, microphone and transmitter in the interview room where I knew he was going to conduct the lineup. I watched it on my phone in my car while it was going on. Once I saw what he'd done, that's when I knew I'd have to quit."

"And where is this recording you made now?"

"I believe you have a copy. I have a copy."

"Did you provide one to the chief of police or the district attorney?"

"I did not."

"Why?"

"I didn't say anything to the chief because I knew I was leaving and I didn't want to put him in the middle.

He's a good man. I didn't provide anything to the district attorney because I knew he wouldn't want it. He'd already made up his mind he was prosecuting this case no matter what. I'd heard conversations between him and Investigator Riddle."

"Objection!" Armstrong said. "How can he know what was in my mind?"

"Sustained," Judge Neese said.

"So instead of blowing the whistle, you just quit the police force."

"I did both. I quit the force and gave a copy of the tape to your representative."

"Right, and we're about to play it."

"I object to this," Armstrong said. "I haven't had a chance to see it."

"Again, a copy of the tape was in the material I provided to Mr. Armstrong when I filed this motion," I said. "And again, he obviously didn't watch it."

"Overruled," Judge Neese said. "Let's see what you have, Mr. Dillard."

For the next several minutes, everyone in the courtroom sat in stunned silence while the oversized monitor on the wall broadcasted the photo lineup in which Investigator Riddle pointed out which players he wanted Sheila Self to choose and then coached her into saying she was one hundred percent certain that the players she'd chosen from the lineup were the same players who dragged her into a bathroom and raped her. I looked over at Armstrong when the tape was almost finished. His face had taken on an odd shade of pink, and a drop of sweat had formed at his right temple.

When the tape was over, I said, "Answer any questions the district attorney might have, please."

Armstrong stood, took a deep breath, and said, "So you've gone from being a police detective to being a rat. Congratulations."

"At least I'm not a criminal like you and Riddle," Marshall said.

"Enough," the judge said.

Attababy, I thought.

Armstrong knew he was screwed. He looked up at the judge and said, "The State is willing to concede this photo lineup was unconstitutional, your Honor. We agree it should be excluded, however, that does not prevent our victim from making identifications in the courtroom at trial."

"There isn't going to be a trial," I said beneath my breath.

"Very well," the judge said. "The identification is excluded. Mr. Dillard, next witness."

"Call Investigator Bo Riddle," I said.

"Your Honor, what's the point?" Armstrong said. "You've already excluded the line-up."

"I think we all deserve to see just how much regard Investigator Riddle has for the judicial process and this court in particular," I said.

I desperately wanted Riddle on the stand because I knew he was a hothead and I knew he would commit perjury. I wasn't sure exactly what would wind up coming out of his mouth, but it wouldn't be good for Armstrong, and I wanted the judge to hear what he had to say while he was under oath.

"Will Investigator Riddle's testimony be relevant to your motion besides the exclusion of the line-up?" Judge Neese said.

"I think your Honor will find his testimony both compelling and enlightening," I said.

"Bring Investigator Riddle in," she said to the bailiff at the door.

Riddle came in looking like an upright turtle. His head was small and slick, and his brown jacket was too tight and his sleeves too short. He'd obviously put on quite a bit of weight and hadn't bothered to adjust his wardrobe accordingly.

He sat down and took the oath. I decided to go right after him.

"Investigator Riddle, the first time you interviewed my client, Kevin Davidson, you kneed him in the groin, didn't you?"

He wasn't expecting the question, and I could tell it threw him.

"That's ridiculous," he said. "If he told you that, he's a liar."

"Your former partner just testified that he witnessed you do it," I said.

"Then he's a liar, too."

"Of course he is. Everyone but you is a liar, I'm sure. Investigator Riddle, are you familiar with the report Officer Tonya James filed the morning after she took Sheila Self, the alleged victim in this case, to the hospital?"

"I don't think I ever read it," he said.

"Well, you probably should have, because it basically says that Ms. Self was pretty much incoherent when she first picked her up, but upon learning she was going to the mental health center, Ms. Self began to claim she'd been raped by multiple attackers. She could not, however, identify any of her attackers."

"She identified them later," Riddle said.

"Right, at a photo lineup that you arranged, correct?"

"That's correct."

"Was there anyone else present at this lineup besides you and Ms. Self?"

"Not that I recall."

"Would you describe for the court exactly how you conducted the lineup?"

Riddle went into a lengthy description of how he painstakingly put together several photo arrays that he showed to Sheila Self. He said he included white men, black men and Latino men of different ages. He showed Ms. Self the photos in groups of six. Over a two-hour time period, he said, she eventually picked out the three players who had been charged. Every word out of his mouth was a lie, everyone in the courtroom knew it, and he was in it up to his ears. I watched Judge Neese as he testified and could imagine the steam coming from her ears.

When he was finished, I said, "Not a single thing you just said was true. You showed her six photos, all of them black football players in uniform, and you showed her which players to pick. You told her you needed to hear from her that she was one hundred percent sure about the identifications. Did you do it because you had some kind of crush on Ms. Self and wanted to make her think you were helping her or are you just a stone-cold racist? I'm betting you're a racist."

Riddle looked at Armstrong for help and then at the judge.

"Are you going to let him get away with calling me a racist?" he said to Judge Neese.

"I'd like to hear what you have to say," the judge said. "Answer the question."

"I conducted a by-the-book, constitutionally-sound lineup, and the victim picked out the defendants," Riddle said.

"Would it surprise you to know that everyone in this courtroom just watched a recording of your constitutionally-sound lineup?" I said. "Your partner at the time, Investigator Marshall, thought you might be a racist. He was concerned about many of the things he'd seen you do and heard you say. So he put a camera in the room where you conducted the lineup. Unusual, don't you think? A police officer clandestinely taping another police officer like that? But you know what, Investigator Marshall's instincts were right. Would you like for me to play the tape again?"

Riddle's cheeks were the color of a firetruck. He looked to be on the verge of having a stroke.

"I'd be happy to play it again. It's been authenticated. Perhaps, after you've watched it, you might want to change your recollection of how you conducted the lineup. Investigator Riddle?"

"That won't be necessary, Mr. Dillard," Judge Neese said. "I don't believe Mr. Armstrong will proceed with a perjury charge against Investigator Riddle, but I can charge him with contempt summarily. Investigator Riddle, I find you in criminal contempt of this court in the presence of the court for willfully committing perjury and for willfully interfering in the process of justice. The maximum amount of time I can put you in jail is ten days and the maximum amount I can fine you is fifty dollars. I wish I could do more, but the law says I can't. Both of those punishments are ordered. Bailiff, take Investigator Riddle into custody and have him taken to jail. Investigator Riddle, don't ever bother coming into my courtroom again because I won't believe a word you say. I also plan to call Chief Starring and tell him what you've done. I'm going to recommend that he terminate your employment because you've been untruthful and I believe you to be a racist. Take him away."

As the bailiff was cuffing Riddle, he looked over at me and said, "I'll be out in ten days, Dillard, and I'll be looking for you."

"That's another count of criminal contempt for threatening defense counsel," the judge said. "You'll be out in twenty days. Open your mouth again and we'll make it thirty."

"I know what you did at my house," I said. "I'll be waiting."

The bailiff led Riddle away. He didn't say anything else, but he didn't have to. The way he was looking at me said it all.

Once he was out of the courtroom, the judge said, "I think we need a little break. Let's recess for fifteen minutes."

"Your honor," I said. "There is a matter I'd like to take up with you in chambers."

"Ten minutes," she said. "You and Mr. Armstrong only."

THURSDAY, OCTOBER 17

en minutes later, Armstrong and I were sitting in front of Judge Neese in her chambers.

"What's on your mind, Mr. Dillard?" she said.

"I'm hoping to end this right now, without having to go back out there and present any more evidence," I said. "I have several more witnesses, one of whom is Dr. Kershaw. I'm sure you know him."

"I do," the judge said. "He usually testifies for the prosecution."

"We sent a sample of Ms. Self's blood to a laboratory that Dr. Kershaw uses regularly. They conducted a Drug Facilitated Sexual Assault analysis of the blood. It's a test the TBI lab isn't set up to do, but the bottom line is that Dr. Kershaw is going to testify that Ms. Self had alcohol, ecstasy and a large amount of GHB in her blood the night she claims she was raped. His expert opinion is that she would have been suffering from anterograde amnesia. She wouldn't have remembered a thing. When you combine that with what Officer James wrote in her report, the videotape that was taken by Laurie Ingram, and the fact that the TBI's DNA analysis showed there was no DNA from any ETSU football player on or in Ms.

Self, it becomes pretty clear that no rape occurred. Oh, and by the way, Mr. Armstrong ran the same test on the blood and failed to provide a copy of the results to me during discovery."

"All of this is a matter for the jury," Armstrong said.

"You might want to be quiet for a minute," I said to Armstrong. I looked back at the judge. "I kept asking myself why Mr. Armstrong was prosecuting this case. He was being totally unreasonable. I didn't think he was a racist, although I'd suspected Riddle was for some time. But now I know why Mr. Armstrong continued with this, and we can either go back into open court and I can embarrass and humiliate him, or we can work this out in chambers, he can ask you to dismiss the case, and everyone can start moving on from this disaster."

Armstrong turned to me and said, "You're so damned smug. You say you know why I'm continuing with this case? You don't know anything. I'm continuing with this case because a young woman made an accusation of rape and it is my job to prosecute crimes in this district."

"You're being blackmailed by a woman named Erlene Barlowe," I said.

Armstrong's neck twitched as though he'd had some kind of involuntary muscle spasm.

"I don't know anyone named Erlene Barlowe," he said.

"Yes, you do, and I can prove it. I can also prove how she's blackmailing you. Do you want me to play the tape I have of her telling me about your affair? I subpoenaed her, too. Surely you had to wonder why I'd do that. I'll put her on the witness stand and play the tape I have of her describing how she's blackmailing you. It's as good or better than the Riddle tape."

"Talk to me, Mr. Dillard," Judge Neese said, pointing at herself. "What's this about an affair and why would it matter?"

"Don't take this wrong," I said. "Personally, I couldn't care less about Mr. Armstrong's sexual orientation, but he's having an affair with an electrician named Michael Adams. It's a long story, judge, but Ms. Barlowe set this entire thing up. She owns the escort service that sent Ms. Self to the party. Her plan was to make a false allegation of rape against a player and then get a big check out of the university. She had no idea Ms. Self and Riddle would turn it into a gang rape and a racial matter, but because they did, Ms. Barlowe stood to get even more money out of the university. Mr. Armstrong has continued to prosecute – even though he had no evidence and knew the allegations were totally false – because Ms. Barlowe threatened to expose his affair with Mr. Adams to the public. And she'd do it, too. She also promised him a little cut of the money. How much was it, Mr. Armstrong? Two hundred grand?"

Judge Neese looked at Armstrong.

"Is this true?" she said.

He started to answer, but suddenly, he burst into tears. He sobbed uncontrollably for a full minute. It was so pitiful I almost felt sorry for him. Almost.

"I'm sorry," he said when he finally composed himself. "I haven't slept in weeks. I just haven't known what to do. I love the job and I want to continue as the district attorney. Can't we put a lid on this Barlowe woman?"

"Wait a minute," Judge Neese said. "I'm far less concerned with Ms. Barlowe than I am with you, Mr. Armstrong. What's been described here, even with the blackmail, is an egregious breach of ethics. Everything you've done in this case screams of prosecutorial misconduct. I'll have to report you to the Board of Professional Responsibility. If I don't, then I'll be in breach of my duty as a judge. You're probably going to lose your license to practice law, and if the FBI gets wind of this, and I'm going to make sure they do, you could be facing an official misconduct charge."

"Please don't do that, your Honor," Armstrong said as the tears started to flow again. "I made a mistake and I regret it. I've regretted it every day since Ms. Barlowe first came to me and told me what she was planning. I just didn't see any way out."

"You're a prosecutor," the judge said. "You should have involved law enforcement. You could have wired yourself up and stung her, which is apparently what Mr. Dillard has done."

"And let everyone know I'm bisexual? That I'm having an affair with a man? I didn't see that as an option."

"So instead, you allowed three young black men to be arrested, kicked out of school, kicked off of the football team, falsely accused of kidnapping and rape, humiliated in front of the entire country, be incarcerated and have their lives put in jeopardy. You gave interviews to news outlets all over the country and tried to set yourself up as a hero. You can sit there and cry all you want, Mr.

Armstrong. You have to accept the consequences of your choices and your actions."

A long silence followed, with the exception of Armstrong's sniffling.

"Where do we go from here?" I said quietly.

"As soon as Mr. Armstrong pulls himself together, we're going back into court."

We waited a few more minutes before Armstrong was able to gather himself. His eyes were red and anyone who took a close look at him would be able to tell he'd been crying, but at that point, I didn't feel the least bit sorry for him. The judge was right. He'd brought every bit of this on himself. Armstrong had allowed a terrible injustice to occur. Not only had he allowed it to occur, he was an active participant. I didn't think things would go well for him when we got back to the courtroom, and I didn't think they'd go well for him in the future.

When we finally walked out, everyone in the courtroom stood as the bailiff called court back into session. I took a seat at the defense table and Kevin said, "How'd it go?"

"We're about to find out," I said.

Judge Neese was flipping through the motion I'd filed. She looked up over her reading glasses a couple of times, sighed heavily, and finally spoke.

"Will the defendants and the prosecution please stand?" she said. "Mr. Dillard, after having heard the testimony presented earlier and after the meeting that just took place in chambers, the court finds that the prosecution of these three young men has, indeed, been in bad faith. It has been nefarious, selective, arbitrary, and, frankly, one of the most egregious examples of prosecutorial misconduct I've ever seen. The defendants' rights under the Fourteenth Amendment have been violated. They have been denied due process. I want to say on the record that this court finds that not only are these young men innocent, but no crime was, in fact, committed. There was no kidnapping. There was no rape. This court will do everything in its power to see that Mr. Armstrong is disbarred and never practices law again. I will also do everything in my power to make sure that Investigator Riddle never works as a law enforcement officer again. I will encourage the Johnson City chief of police to pursue a false report investigation against the alleged victim.

"I know this case has caused deep racial division at a time when racial division was the last thing this community, or any community for that matter, needed. My hope is that the resolution of this case will help to calm the waters a bit and that we can get back to the business of respecting each other and doing what is right in our criminal justice system. Mr. Davidson, Mr. Wright, Mr. Belle, the court orders the cases against each of you dismissed with prejudice. That means you cannot ever be prosecuted for these crimes that didn't happen, no matter what, and again, I want to emphasize on the record that this court specifically finds that *these crimes did not happen.* You are free to go. Bailiff, call the jail and have Mr. Wright's and Mr. Belle's personal effects sent over here immediately. I don't want them to spend another second in jail. If they don't have transportation, I would ask that their lawyers arrange or provide transportation. They can wait in the jury room until their clothing and other effects arrive, change out of those jail uniforms, and leave. Mr. Davidson, Mr. Wright, Mr. Belle, I apologize to each and every one of you for the pain you have endured. If I'd known earlier what I know now, I would have put a stop to this. Court is in recess."

THURSDAY, OCTOBER 17

In the parking lot, Leon Bates heard from one of the bailiffs posted inside that the hearing was over and what had happened. It was, to say the least, tense in the parking lot surrounding the Justice Center in Jonesborough. Leon instructed the bailiff to keep everyone inside until he gave the all clear.

Leon's men had been able to scoop up two pick-up trucks with four men each in them at the power station based about five miles from the courthouse based on information provided by Sarah Dillard's friend, Greg Murray, early that morning. The men were all armed with fully-automatic assault rifles, but Leon's deputies had been waiting for them, surprised them, and arrested them without a shot being fired. Still, the arrests confirmed Leon's worst fears. Some kind of attack was planned that day.

At the courthouse, however, the kind of security Leon needed to provide was a nightmare. The courthouse faced a busy four-lane highway between Johnson City and Greeneville. If one walked out the front door, Tavern Hill Road was just to the left. Leon had blocked that road off three miles away at Hairetown Road, but he couldn't just shut down Highway 11E, which was the four-lane that ran parallel to the courthouse in the front.

Across the highway, there were three feeder streets – N. Cherokee St., N. 2nd Ave. and Washington Ave. – that could be used as a means of approach by someone with hostile intentions. Leon had checkpoints on both sides of 11E, on the old Jonesborough Highway, on Main Street, on Old State Route 34, and on Highway 81, but his officers couldn't force people to get out and allow their vehicles to be searched without some reasonable suspicion that they had committed or were about to commit a crime. Three or four men in a pick-up – white or black – did not provide that suspicion. And even so, with a fairly simple plan – like being in a home or a hotel or one of the restaurants or diners close to the courthouse and mobilizing quickly – Leon knew small groups could get to the courthouse parking lot, and if they did, all hell could break loose.

He had snipers on the roof of the courthouse and on the roofs of two businesses across the street. He had his men and vehicles placed tactically so that it would be very, very difficult for anyone to get to the courthouse itself. But if they came from opposite directions, got into the parking lot, and wanted to start shooting at each other or at Leon's men, there would be little he could do but shoot back.

Less than five minutes after Leon was notified the hearing was over, he saw a red SUV, followed by a blue pick-up truck, pull slowly into the courthouse driveway. They'd come from the west, his right, and they stopped fifty feet short of Leon's SWAT team, who were set up behind concrete barricades that had been hauled into the site.

A minute later, two more pick-ups, both silver, pulled in from the east and parked at the edge of the lot stopping short of a Tennessee Highway Patrol SWAT team. The men in the vehicles that had come from the west were black. The men who had come from the east were white. Leon counted what he thought to be eight whites and eight blacks. He saw weapons in the vehicles. Men were starting to get out of the vehicles and take cover on the sides, behind the doors, behind the trucks, in the truck beds. Leon pushed a button on his communications microphone and said, "Hold your fire, gents. Go easy."

Leon quickly reached into the SUV he'd driven to the courthouse that morning and grabbed a bullhorn. He set the Colt M4A1 carbine he was carrying in the back seat and climbed on top of the SUV. He was wearing full tactical gear, but he was exposed. A head shot could kill him. There were also certain types of armor piercing bullets available. He hoped none of these people were quite that sophisticated. Still, Leon stood atop the SUV and faced them. He had to try to settle this peacefully.

"The hearing is over!" Leon said through the bullhorn. "The right thing happened in there. The boys who were falsely charged have been exonerated and will be released. A police officer has been taken to jail and the district attorney will end up being disbarred. There is no need for any bloodshed, no need for any more hatred. The system has finally worked.

"Now if you men turn around and drive on out of here right now, we won't even follow you. We'll let you go. No harm has been done. It's over! Do you hear me? There is nothing you can do here but spread more hatred and fear and blood, and there's just no sense in it. No sense at all. So please, I'm asking you. Hell, I'm begging you. Load up your weapons, get back in your vehicles, and drive away."

THURSDAY, OCTOBER 17

The attorneys, boys and I all gathered in the jury room off a hallway outside the courtroom. The boys looked stunned.

"What in the world happened back there in chambers?" Jim Beaumont asked me.

I winked at him and said, "I'll never tell."

Kevin thanked me and Charlie and Jack over and over. He had questions: "Does this mean I get my life back? Will they let me finish school? Do you think we'll get to play the last few games of the season? What do we do now?"

A bailiff came to the door and told us to stay in the jury room until he gave the all clear. His name was Hobie Beales, and I'd known him for more than twenty years. I walked up to him and said quietly, "What's going on out there, Hobie?"

"Might be trouble brewing," he said.

I nodded at him, and told him I'd be coming out in a minute.

"I don't think that'd be a good idea, counselor," he said. "We picked up a couple of truckloads of boys earlier. Sheriff thinks there's gonna be bad trouble."

"I'll be out," I said. "Don't shoot me."

"You get shot, it'll be of your own accord," Hobie said. "Don't say I didn't warn you."

I turned to Jack and Charlie.

"Stay in here no matter what. Lock these doors down. The bailiffs are all armed with rifles and shotguns today, nobody's going to get past them. I'm going to go see what's going on outside."

"Dad," Jack said. "Why don't you just stay back here with us?"

"Because Leon's out there, and Leon's my friend."

"But you don't even have a weapon."

"I hope I won't need one. I'll be back in a minute."

I went out the door and jogged down the hall. I turned a corner and went through a door that led to the lobby. I could see Leon outside standing on top of a department issue SUV. I couldn't quite make out what he was saying through the thick glass that ran all along the front of the building, but suddenly, a lone shot rang out and Leon went flying off the top of the SUV and landed on the asphalt. Everything went into slow-motion as I felt myself yelling, "No!" and I began to run toward the front door.

When I hit the door with my shoulder, a cacophony of small arms fire, assault rifles, mostly, was building to a crescendo similar to that at the climax of a holiday fireworks display. Bullets were whistling, smashing glass, tearing into metal vehicles, skipping off the asphalt pavement.

Leon was lying in the fetal position on the asphalt about thirty feet outside the door. I made my way to him quickly while the firefight raged around me. I pulled him up close under the SUV and looked at his flak jacket. There was a tear, but no blood, and upon further inspection, the ceramic tile backed by Kevlar had held. Leon had been hit by a high-powered round. He'd be in a lot of pain, but he was alive and would be okay. He moaned and opened his eyes.

"Damn," he said. "Damn. Some son of a bitch broke my ribs, brother."

I pulled him closer to shield him further from the bullets that were still whizzing, albeit more infrequently.

"Where the hell is your weapon?" I said.

"It's on the seat."

The gunfire was beginning to slow. I stuck my head up and looked around. Police officers were advancing on vehicles on both ends of the parking lot. The vehicles had been shot full of holes. I could see bodies lying in pools of blood. There were men writhing and screaming. It reminded me of a time many years ago on Grenada when my Ranger battalion jumped onto Point Salines airstrip. It was a time I didn't want to think about.

"It's almost over, Leon," I said. "Your guys have them. Their vehicles are too damaged to move. Nobody's getting away."

"I tried to stop it," Leon said. There was pain in his eyes. "I swear it, brother Dillard. I tried to stop it."

"I'm sure you did. A lot of people tried to stop it. This isn't your fault."

"We've got a mass shooting in my county caused by a woman I got too close to. This is on me."

"There'll be plenty of room for blame later," I said. "For now, let me see if we can't get you on your feet. You're the sheriff. Stand up and act like one."

Leon smiled and looked at me with a sparkle in his eye. I could tell he was grateful I came out to help him.

"Don't be giving me a hard time," he said as I helped him to his feet. "Look at you. Who comes to a firefight in a damned suit and tie?"

THURSDAY, OCTOBER 17

I turned Leon over to the medics and went back inside. As I went through the front door, I looked back over my shoulder. It truly did resemble a military mop-up operation out in front of the courthouse. A helicopter had landed on the front lawn beyond the parking lot, there were medical personnel everywhere, blue lights flashing, police and dogs, and there was blood. A lot of blood.

I wondered whether everyone had gotten what they came for. Several men had apparently ridden in on a wave of hatred and adrenaline, inspired by events that didn't concern them, determined only to kill either a policeman or someone with a different skin color. Several of them, it was obvious, had paid the ultimate price.

The bailiffs were beginning to release people from the courtroom. They were ordering them to proceed straight to their vehicles and to leave the courthouse immediately. That included the media. The media was told they could go across the street, drive up and down Highway 11-E, or observe from the shopping center across Tavern Hill Road. There would be a press conference later. Everyone else was told the best thing they could do was to get as far away from the courthouse as possible as quickly as possible.

I went back into the jury room. Jack and Charlie and the rest of the people I'd left ten minutes earlier were still there.

"The bailiff said you went running right into the middle of it," Jack said. "He said you could have gotten yourself killed."

"Leon was hit," I said. "I just went to make sure he was okay, and he is. I think it's over, but let's get out of here."

The four of us – Charlie, Jack, Kevin and I – gathered our things and walked out of the jury room, down the hall, through the door, into the lobby, where we were met by Kevin's parents and three other members of his family. Mr. Davidson shook my hand and thanked me.

"You don't need to thank me," I said. "He didn't do anything wrong."

"That's just it. He didn't do anything wrong, but if it hadn't been for you, he could have wound up in prison for the rest of his life."

"Well, instead he's going to finish up the school year and head off to law school. The best thing you can do, all of you, is put this behind you. I'm not saying forget it because you won't, but put it behind you, hold your heads up, and move on with your lives. Are you going to be in town for a couple of days?"

"We'll probably leave tomorrow."

"Stop by the office early and we'll rehash some things. I'll tell you what went on in the judge's chambers."

"We'll be there," he said, and we all turned and walked toward the door.

It happened before I could get out the front door.

It happened so quickly there was nothing I could do.

I was in the back of the group. Kevin's family went out, followed by Kevin, then Charlie. Jack was a few feet behind her, and I was behind him. As soon as Kevin cleared the doorway, I saw a woman move out quickly from behind a pillar to my right and run straight toward him. A flash of steel caught the sunlight as she raised a large knife over her head. I opened my mouth to yell a warning, but it was too late. Kevin had already turned to his left, following his family to their car. Charlie spotted her, and she threw herself between the attacker and Kevin. The knife came down, and Charlie reached up and tried to block it. I saw the knife bury itself deeply into Charlie's left forearm, and she yelled out in pain. Sheila withdrew the knife and raised it again just as Jack realized what was happening. Before I could get through the door, and before Sheila could make another strike, Jack had bull-rushed Sheila, lifted her onto his shoulder in a fireman's carry, and slammed her onto the concrete sidewalk so hard I could hear her skull crack. She lay motionless on the walk, her eyes open, seemingly staring at the sky above. The move Jack used on her was one I'd taught him many years earlier. I'd seen him use it before, but never on a woman, and never with such devastating effect. He was so strong, and apparently had experienced such a rush of adrenaline, that Sheila looked like a rag doll.

I rushed through the door to Charlie, who was standing with a gaping wound in her arm. I walked her over to a concrete column and sat her on the ground. A bailiff came rushing over, his pistol drawn.

"Get us some medics," I said. "Hurry!"

Jack stood over Sheila for a few seconds, seemingly in a daze. He finally came out of it and moved quickly to Charlie and me.

"Charlie, I'm so sorry," he said. "I couldn't get to her."

I took my tie off and began wrapping it tightly around Charlie's arm. I was terrified. The wound was oozing dark blood. It was right in the middle of the underside of her forearm, about four inches up from the base of her hand, and I was afraid the knife may have struck either or both of the radial or ulnar arteries. If it had severed them or opened them up, she could bleed to death.

The medics showed up in less than a minute. I stood back and got out of their way. Two of them immediately went to work on Charlie, while two more went to work on Sheila Self.

"I killed her," Jack said. "I think I killed her."

"Take it easy," I said. "You did what you had to do."

The medics slowed the bleeding from Charlie's arm fairly quickly. I didn't notice any blood spraying; it wasn't gushing, which, to me, meant no artery had been sliced or severed. She did have a nasty gash, though, and they immediately set about cleaning and dressing the wound. A few minutes later, they loaded her into an ambulance. Jack climbed in with her, and they drove off to the Johnson City Medical Center.

I stayed and watched while they worked on Sheila. They tried to stop the ever-widening pool of blood oozing from her skull. She went into cardiac arrest shortly after I began watching, and they were unsuccessful in reviving her. They finally stopped working on her fifteen minutes after they started and covered her body with a sheet.

Sheila Self, the woman who had set all of the wheels in motion at the direction of Erlene Barlowe, was dead, and my son had killed her. I knew there wouldn't be legal repercussions – he had killed her in defense of another – but I also knew Jack. Psychologically, he would be in for a long, rough road ahead.

THURSDAY, OCTOBER 17

We gathered at our house that evening. Lilly had been following the case on the news and I spoke to her on the phone for an hour. Charlie spent a couple of hours in the Emergency Room at the hospital before they let her go. I went by briefly. It was like a scene from a war movie in there with bullet-riddled bodies being carted in and wheeled off to surgery.

We stayed glued to the news. They were reporting that thirteen of the sixteen men who opened fire on each other and the police had been shot and killed. The police were identifying bodies and notifying next of kin. Only two police officers, besides Leon, were wounded. One received a superficial wound when his neck was barely grazed by a bullet. Another inch toward his neck and he would have likely been dead. The other was struck in the knee when a bullet somehow found its way through a tiny gap in his body armor. He was in stable condition at the hospital.

Around 11:00 p.m., a face flashed across the television screen that gave me pause. It was the black man who had come to our office and threatened me with the Clint Eastwood hand cannon. They reported that his name was originally Jamie Lynn Greenlee, from Atlanta. He'd done a lengthy prison term for selling crack cocaine and shooting another dealer. At some point along the way, he converted to Islam and changed his name to Kareem Abdul Mohammed. He was a member of the New Black Panther Party, they said.

No more radical rantings and ravings for you, my friend, I thought as they moved on to the next dead radical. *Now you're just another dead hate monger.*

One thing the television news station did well was gauge the reaction of the community. To say the people of Northeast Tennessee were shocked by what had happened in our own back yard was an understatement. There was genuine disbelief that the racial animus in our community ran so deeply. It appeared that people were willing to take a serious look in the mirror and take some steps to try and bridge the gaps of ignorance and intolerance that allowed such things to happen. For my part, I was ashamed of what had happened. I was ashamed that I couldn't put a stop to it. I was ashamed that so much hatred was so close to the surface in our community.

Around eleven thirty I asked Jack to take a walk outside with me. He'd been quiet and sullen all evening, and I knew he was thinking about Sheila Self.

We put on jackets and walked out into a breezy, chilly night. A new moon was almost directly overhead, the sky dappled with fast-moving cumulus clouds.

"You want to talk about it?" I said as we walked slowly toward the trail where I jogged.

"I don't know," he said. "Doesn't seem like there's much to talk about. What's done is done."

"How do you feel?"

"Guilty. Sad. Stupid. I could have handled it a dozen different ways. I didn't have to body slam her like that."

"She'd just stabbed the woman you love and was about to take another crack at her," I said. "You reacted. You didn't think because you didn't have time to think. You just reacted. I'm sorry you took a life, Jack. It isn't a club I would ever want you to join. But you did. You killed her. There was no wrong in it."

"I could have taken that knife away from her," he said. "I could have arm-barred her. I could have choked her until she was unconscious."

"Maybe. Maybe not. Maybe she throws the damned knife into your eye. Maybe she slices you with it before you can take it and you wind up bleeding to death. Maybe she gets it into Charlie's chest the second time she tries. None of those things happened because you reacted the way you did. You were decisive. You saw the danger and you eliminated it."

"I didn't intend to eliminate it permanently. Or at least I don't think I did. That's what is bothering me the most right now. Maybe I *did* intend to kill her. When I saw that knife go into Charlie's arm, I think I may have formed the intent right there on the spot."

"It happens," I said. "How much am I going to have to worry about you?"

"You have enough to worry about with Mom."

"I'm serious. Do you think you need to see a shrink? We'll do whatever we need to do to get you past this."

"How did you handle it, Dad?"

I thought about it before responding. I'd always been one to bottle up feelings, to channel emotions, especially those that were highly stressful. There'd been times in my life when that approach wasn't healthy. I wanted to help him avoid the mistakes I'd made.

"The men I killed in Grenada were soldiers. I was a soldier."

"How many did you kill?" he said.

"Three. I shot two and took one out with a grenade. I looked at them up close after I shot them. It wasn't like it was impersonal, but I was duty-bound. They were trying to kill me, too. It bothered me for a while, I've had nightmares about it, but I don't dwell on it and I never have. I just decided to accept what happened, not feel guilty, and move on. Then John Lipscomb sent the *sicarios*, and I killed five of them protecting my home and family. I've never really given that a second thought. I did what I had to do under the circumstances. I survived, barely, and I protected the people I loved. Once it was over, it was over. I let it go. And that's what you have to do. You have to let it go. You can't let it eat at you. If you do, you'll find yourself having some serious problems."

"So I just let it go? Sounds easier said than done."

"Talk about it if you need to. Talk to Charlie, talk to me, talk to your mom. But try not to dwell on it. Eventually, the guilt will fade, the memory will fade. It will always be with you. It'll always be on the fringes of your mind, but it doesn't have to have a serious negative impact on your life."

"I keep hearing the sound her head made when it hit the concrete," he said.

I knew what he meant. That same sound had stayed with me, too.

"The sound will fade with the memory. Think about where you're going, Jack, not about where you've been. Learning from the past is one thing. Wallowing in it is another. I know you. You're too strong mentally to let this paralyze you. Think about how much Charlie needs you. Think about how much your Mom needs you. Think about how much I need you. And then remind yourself how much we all love you. We'll get through this, son. You're not alone. We'll get through it together."

He turned his head toward me as we continued down the path.

"I'll be all right," he said.

"Yes, yes you will."

"Do you know how much I love you, Dad?"

I nodded.

"I do, Jack."

"I still think you're crazy, but I love you."

TUESDAY, OCTOBER, 22

A light snow, the first of the year, began to fall as Caroline and I headed into the mountains west of Knoxville on our latest trip to Nashville for her immunotherapy. She was doing relatively well, all things considered, and I was feeling relieved after being able to climb out of the pressure cooker that had been the ETSU rape case that wasn't a rape at all.

"I don't think I ever told you how proud I was of you," Caroline said as her car climbed steadily along Interstate 40.

"Proud of me for what?"

"For taking on that case in the first place. For believing in those boys. For having the courage to take on racists from both sides. And for making sure it turned out right."

"It didn't turn out right for everybody," I said.

"It shouldn't have turned out right for some of them. Karma's tough on some people."

Judge Neese had been true to her word. The Tennessee Supreme Court had suspended Mike Armstrong's law license pending disbarment proceedings in front of the Board of Professional Responsibility.

An assistant district attorney named Tony Brooks had been appointed to serve in the interim, pending the primary election the following April. No one had seen or heard from Armstrong since he received notice of his suspension, but the newspaper had reported that the feds had opened an official misconduct investigation. Since Erlene didn't actually pay him any money, he might beat the charge, but he'd certainly be sweating – or crying – for several months to come. I didn't really give a damn what happened to him. He'd done a great deal of damage, and he deserved every bit of what was coming.

The most shocking thing that came of the hearing – outside the bloodbath that occurred afterward – was that Bo Riddle hanged himself in his jail cell three days after Judge Neese held him in contempt. I suppose he knew the real hammer would come down on him sooner or later. Leon Bates had discovered videotape of the truck that was at my house the night the cross was burned. The feds had moved in and turned up the heat on his buddies that were captured at the power station, among them Garrett Brown. All of them were facing a variety of federal firearms charges along with attempted civil rights intimidation charges. One or two of them apparently had made deals and agreed to testify against Riddle. He must have known he was on his way to a federal penitentiary when he slipped the sheet around his neck. I worried about Greg Murray, Sarah's boyfriend, a little. Even if Garrett Brown and his white supremacist buddies went off to the penitentiary for a while, they'd most likely be back in five years and Greg might have to deal with them. They had to know it was him who gave them up.

All three of the players: Kevin Davidson, Devonte Wright and Evan Belle, were allowed to return to school and the football team. They had classroom work to catch up on and they had to get back into shape, but the last time I talked to Kevin, he seemed genuinely satisfied with the way things were going. He and the other boys had retained civil attorneys to deal with the university. ETSU wouldn't be paying Erlene Barlowe, but they'd been putting out some money for the three young men they condemned before they were given their day in court.

As for Erlene Barlowe, Leon had decided to leave her alone. He didn't want erotic videotapes of himself and Erlene being distributed throughout the state, and he figured Erlene had been punished enough because everything had gone so terribly wrong. Sheila was dead, along with several men. There had been a lot of property damaged or destroyed at the courthouse and at my house. The university was paying – they just weren't paying her. So Erlene was still free to ply her trade and prey on lonely perverts and druggies.

"Thank you," I said to Caroline. "What you think of me means more than anything else."

She reached over and took my hand as the snow began to fall harder. It was beautiful against the backdrop of the mountains.

"You're a good guy, Joe Dillard," Caroline said. "I'm glad we found each other all those years ago."

"Me, too," I said as I turned to her, smiled and winked. "And we still have a long way to go."

Thank you for reading, and I sincerely hope you enjoyed *Due Process*. As an independently published author, I rely on you, the reader, to spread the word. So if you enjoyed the book, please tell your friends and family, and if it isn't too much trouble, I would appreciate a brief review on Amazon. Thanks again. My best to you and yours.

Scott

ABOUT THE AUTHOR

Scott Pratt was born in South Haven, Michigan, and moved to Tennessee when he was thirteen years old. He is a veteran of the United States Air Force and holds a Bachelor of Arts degree in English from East Tennessee State University and a Doctor of Jurisprudence from the University of Tennessee College of Law. He lives in Northeast Tennessee with his wife, their dogs, and a parrot named JoJo.

www.scottprattfiction.com

ALSO BY SCOTT PRATT

An Innocent Client (Joe Dillard #1)
In Good Faith (Joe Dillard #2)
Injustice for All (Joe Dillard #3)
Reasonable Fear (Joe Dillard #4)
Conflict of Interest (Joe Dillard #5)
Blood Money (Joe Dillard #6)
A Crime of Passion (Joe Dillard #7)
Judgment Cometh (And That Right Soon) (Joe Dillard #8)
Justice Redeemed (Darren Street #1)
Justice Burning (Darren Street #2)
Justice Lost (Darren Street #3)
River on Fire

Made in United States
Orlando, FL
04 September 2023

36686928R00165